8/ SPACE RACE

Other Avon Camelot Books in the
GONERS *Series by*
Jamie Simons and E.W. Scollon

Coming Soon

Visit *Goners* on the Web at
www.goners.com

GONERS

8/ SPACE RACE

JAMIE SIMONS
and E.W. SCOLLON

Illustrations by MICHAEL EVANS

AN AVON CAMELOT BOOK

This is a work of fiction. Names, characters, places, and incidents either are the product of the author's imagination or are used fictitiously. Any resemblance to actual events, locales, organizations, or persons, living or dead, is entirely coincidental and beyond the intent of either the author or the publisher.

AVON BOOKS, INC.
1350 Avenue of the Americas
New York, New York 10019

Copyright © 1999 by Jamie S. Simons and E.W. Scollon, Jr.
Interior illustrations copyright © 1998 by Michael Evans
Interior illustrations by Michael Evans
Published by arrangement with the authors
Library of Congress Catalog Card Number: 98-93658
ISBN: 0-380-79737-2
www.goners.com

First Avon Camelot Printing: March 1999

CAMELOT TRADEMARK REG. U.S. PAT. OFF. AND IN OTHER COUNTRIES, MARCA REGISTRADA, HECHO EN U.S.A.

Printed in the U.S.A.

OPM   10   9   8   7   6   5   4   3   2   1

ACKNOWLEDGMENTS

Thanks to John Hennessy, Emily Hutta, and Lisa Sturz.

1

Gogol

"It's not fair!" I shouted at the rock wall. My voice echoed off the walls of the cavern. "Why me? Why do I have to be a mutant? Why do I have to be a freak? I want to be like everyone else!"

I'd come into the Tunnels to get away from everyone above ground on Planetoid Roma. I needed time to think. Strictly off-limits to students like me, the Tunnels were the one place I knew I could go where I'd be one hundred percent totally alone. Now I found myself screaming at the top of my lungs and pounding on the slime-covered walls, letting out all the frustration of the past few weeks.

Whoosh! The acid geyser behind me erupted with sudden fury. I jumped back and tried to press my body into the rock wall. As the whole stinking mess began to rain down, I realized my only chance was to try and get out of there—and fast.

I skittered along the wall, feeling my way with fingers and toes, while keeping my eyes on the fountain of acid. One false step and I'd be turned to mush. I took giant sideways steps. One. Two. Slide. Slip!

"Aarrgghh!" I screamed, hurtling down a slick tube in total darkness. Twists and turns battered my body, tossing me from side to side. I'd fallen into a giant rock worm tunnel! That meant the rock worm's mouth couldn't be too far away. I lifted my head to look. BASH! Ow! Bad idea. But for an ohno-second I saw the soft phosphorous glow of the beast's lips—wide open. *Can't let it swallow me,* I told myself, trying not to panic. *Put your feet out! Put your feet out!* my mind screamed. I dragged my feet against the wall of the chute. That slowed me down a little. I dragged my hands on the sides, searching for a handhold. Beneath me I could feel the warm, humid breath of the creature, its mouth getting closer! Closer!

Stop!!! I thrust out my legs, using them to wedge myself against the walls of the tube. Then I looked down.

"HELP!" I screamed, knowing full well no one could hear me. The rock worm's greedy jaws were snapping just inches away. What now? Feeling above my head, I managed to find tiny handholds and pull myself up slightly. *Hold on!* I told myself. *Now lift your foot! Kick! Kick! Smash!*

Slowly, the side of the tube cracked and split. Cool air from the tunnels rushed in. The worm started moving in on me. I kicked with all my might and broke open a pretty good-sized hole. Moving my hands carefully, feeling for new handholds, I thrust one leg out through the hole I'd made. *Now the rest of me,* I told myself. With one mighty heave, I pushed myself out of the rock worm's domain. Luckily, my feet hit solid ground outside the tube. *At last,* I thought. But my luck didn't hold. Neither did the crust bubble I was standing on.

"AAAHHHHH!" I screamed as the ground under my feet gave way. I was suddenly tumbling down a steep slope in an avalanche of dirt. *Plop!* I hit bottom and lay on the tunnel floor, trying to catch my breath and clear the worm juice and dirt out of my mouth. I seemed, finally, to be on solid ground, but where?

When I finally felt strong enough to move, I sat up, took out my light stick, and stuck it on the rock ledge over my head. Then I pulled out the map my three friends—Rubi, Xela, and Arms Akimbo—had made. They claimed they'd sneaked into the Tunnels and mapped them just for fun, which didn't make me feel too confident about the map's accuracy. But it was all I had. According to the map, I'd just taken an unscheduled detour to Tunnel Eleven. Now I just had to make my way to the Crisscross and down Tunnel Thirteen.

That's where the others were waiting, in Dr. Autonomou's underground lab. It was from the lab that we'd

3

been running secret missions to Earth. Brushing off my clothes, I peeled the light stick off the ledge and started back down the Tunnel. That's when I heard it. *Ping.* Then again. *Ping.* No doubt about it, I was being followed. And whoever—or whatever—it was could be dangerous, turn me in, end my days on Roma.

I darted off the path and hid myself in the shadow of a boulder. *Ping.* I could see the outline of a life form approaching. I crouched down and waited until just the right moment. Then, I jumped up screaming, "AAARRGGGHHHH!"

2

Arms Akimbo

I was walking through the Tunnels, pretty sure I'd catch up with Gogol at any moment, when something big and scary jumped out of the shadows right in front of me and started screaming!

"AAARRGGGHHH!" I screamed right back at it, waving my four arms over my head. Until I recognized it and stopped right away. "Gogol! You scared me to death!"

"I scared you?" he sputtered. "Why are you following me, Arms?"

"Following? I wouldn't say *following*. More like walking in the same direction. But trailing behind. Of course, I skipped the detour to the acid-spewing bog. I guessed you'd come out here. Pretty good, huh?''

"Uh-huh. And what was that pinging I heard?''

My jaw dropped open. I couldn't believe he'd heard it. I held out my lower left hand and opened my fist. There in the palm of my six-fingered hand was a small pile of silvery rods. "You were hearing pins drop. Amazing.''

"Nothing to it. Comes from my Alzorian side,'' Gogol said. "So what are those things?''

"Locator pins. I was dropping them every so often. Didn't want to get lost.''

Gogol looked around at the green glowing walls dripping with slime. "Can't say I blame you.''

"Why are you down here?'' I asked. "What if you'd gotten lost?''

Gogol held up the map Rubi, Xela, and I had made of the Tunnels. "I was counting on this to get me through.''

"Oh. This is a little late to be telling you this . . . I guess . . . maybe. But the parts on that map that I drew in . . . well. Sometimes I got a little lost. So I kind of sort of made things up as I went along.''

"No wonder you bring locator pins,'' Gogol said.

"Don't leave home without 'em!'' I chirped. "So why are you here?''

"I wanted to be alone.''

"Oops. Guess I sort of messed that up. Want me to get lost?''

6

Gogol smiled. "Hard to do with a trail of pings."

"You know what I mean. Do you want more time alone?"

"No, it's all right," Gogol said. "I was just getting ready to head for Autonomou's lab anyway."

"Then you are really lucky I came along when I did," I said as I took the map out of Gogol's hands and crumpled it up in all four of mine. "This old thing would have never gotten you there."

"Somehow I should have known that," said Gogol.

"Oh, well." I shrugged. "Can't all be perfect." Then taking the lead, I headed for the Crisscross. I named it that. It's the place where all the tunnels under Planetoid Roma come together, then head off in every direction. "Tunnel Thirteen, dead ahead," I said, leaping over a boulder.

"So why were you worried about me, Arms?" Gogol asked. That stopped my leaping. I turned to face him.

"Hmmm . . . why was I worried? Let's see. Why would I be worried? Could it be because you've been just the teensiest bit distant and moody ever since Professor Hal E. Toesis brought you up on trial?"

"Distant?"

"And moody. Every time someone talks to you, you either snap at him or look like your head is a kagillion parsnits away."

"I've had a lot on my mind," Gogol said, pushing past me. He started walking up Tunnel Thirteen so fast I had to run to catch up.

"Hey, didn't mean to hurt your feelings. Of *course*

7

you've had a lot on your mind. Who wouldn't? It's not every day that someone goes up against one of Diplomatic Universal Headquarters' professors in court and reduces him to tears."

"I'm not all that proud of what I did, Arms," Gogol mumbled. "I keep playing it over and over in my mind."

"My point exactly."

Gogol let out a huge sigh. "I mean, let's be honest. Professor Hal E. Toesis had it right. I was guilty of the charges. Guilty of exploring the Tunnels, guilty of traveling to Earth, guilty of—"

"Whoa, Gogol, take it easy. You did what you did for a very good reason."

"Yeah, right. Good try, Arms."

"I mean it," I said as I whirled him around so he had to look straight into my eyes. "You sound like all that was at stake was saving yourself. But if it weren't for you, what would have happened to the Goners?"

"Okay, I'll give you half a point for that argument," Gogol snickered.

"Hey, listen, buster. If you hadn't won that case, all one hundred sixty-eight mission specialists still stranded on Earth would have no hope of ever being rescued. If the High Council had learned the truth, they'd have shut down our secret missions and left the Goners stranded. Again. And what about Dr. Autonomou? She would have been banished from the Planetary Union forever. All those years she spent working in secret to get the wormhole to Earth open again would have been wasted.

8

But go ahead. Feel sorry for yourself if it makes you happy.''

Gogol didn't say anything for a long time. Neither did I. We just walked along in silence. Fine with me. All in all, I thought it was a pretty good speech. No way I was going to ruin the moment.

Finally Gogol looked over at me. "You're a good friend, Arms Akimbo."

"Well, I put up with you," I said, coming over and tickling him in his very Earthling-like ribs.

That actually made Gogol laugh. I hadn't heard that in a while. "Listen," he said. "It takes a good friend to speak the truth. But what you said doesn't make what I'm feeling go away." Gogol let out a huge sigh. "Listen, Arms. I won that case by being dishonest. I didn't lie, but I didn't exactly tell the truth either. I sidestepped the facts, pretended I didn't understand the questions, told only half-truths. And I'm not proud of that."

"I understand," I assured him. And I did. After all, being dishonest is strictly against the Code of Values. All life-forms in the Planetary Union must abide by the Code. It's what makes it possible for the inhabitants of the 127 planets that make up the P.U. to live together in peace. "But you did what you did to save others."

"I know that, Arms. I only wish what was troubling me were so simple."

"So what is it?" I asked.

"It felt so natural to avoid the truth. It was exciting to outwit Toesis. I enjoyed being dishonest. I liked being tricky. I *loved* winning."

"You poor mutant," I said, giving Gogol a four-arm full-press hug. "It must be the Earthling in you coming out." *Wow!* I thought. *That could make living in the P.U. pretty hard.* Competition is a strict no-no. Our leaders say it gets in the way of peace. And Gogol *loved* it? That couldn't be good.

Even worse, Gogol had no one to go to for answers. He was on his own. As far as we knew, he was the only Earthling-Alzorian mutant in existence. No wonder he was desperate to get to the bottom of his strange origin. My guess was, he could have dealt with having no one around who looked like him. But how do you live with having no one who feels what you feel?

Reaching up, I put an arm over Gogol's shoulder. "Maybe a BATH will help."

Gogol smiled. "I know it will. You're still coming, right?"

"Of course! I talked to my parents. They're definitely going to be on a mission during our Break-Away-To-Home. So there's no reason for me to go to Armagettem. Besides, I've never been to Alzor. I can't wait to sklii down Mount Opticus, skklooter across Lake Noendinsite, buy useless trinkets at—"

Gogol started laughing. "Arms, I don't know how to break this to you, but we won't have time for any of that."

"Huh? What do you mean?"

"I'm not going back to relax," Gogol confided. "I'm going back to find out how I got the way I am, once and for all."

"And just how do you propose doing that?"

10

"I don't know exactly. Talk to my parents, check the birth records, do some research."

"Ooohhh, that sounds like fun."

"Arms, you don't have to come. Seriously, I don't mind."

"Good."

That stopped him. "You're not coming?"

I just scowled. "Gogol, do you *really* think I'm going to give up my hard-earned BATH to help you research your family history?"

"Well I . . ."

"Sitting around some stuffy old library when normal life-forms are out having fun?"

Gogol moaned. "What was I thinking?"

"Obviously you weren't thinking at all," I said, trying to look really angry. Then I smiled. "Because you know I'd never let you down!"

"No hard feelings, Arms. . . . You're coming?"

"Are you kidding? Who else is going to keep you out of trouble?" Suddenly Gogol doubled over. "Are you okay?" I asked rushing to his side.

"It's just the—just the—" said Gogol, wheezing with laughter. "The thought of *you,* Arms Akimbo, keeping someone out of trouble."

"Okay," I said as I gently gave him quadruple noogies, "so it's not my strong suit. But I try."

"Don't try too hard." Gogol chuckled. "You're just right the way you are."

I had to admit, he had a point. "I know," I said, and smiled.

11

3

Rubidoux

"They should have been here ikrons ago," Dr. Autonomou said for the umpteenth time. The cave-of-a-lab shook with every step as she paced the floor. No wonder. Dr. A is huge.

"The strange thing," said Xela, "is that both Gogol *and* Arms are missing. What do you think, Rubidoux?"

I looked right into Xela's big yellow eyes—which go nicely with her blue skin—and shot her a "Rubi," my patented, charming smile. "I think you worry too much. They probably just got caught up packing or signing up for next session's classes. Then again, maybe they were

12

abducted by aliens." I thought I'd get a laugh with that one, but no luck. Our school, DUH—Diplomatic Universal Headquarters—is attended by life-forms from all 127 planets of the Planetary Union. The best of the best from all over the P.U. come here. So the place is crawling with aliens!

"I'm afraid I can't wait for them much longer." Xela sighed. "My space roamer to planet Numi leaves soon."

"Maybe they lost their Alleviator keys again," Autonomou grumbled. She had stopped pacing and stood with her hands shoved deep into the pockets of her oversized lab coat.

"I doubt it," Xela said. "Even if one of them had, the other would have a key."

"Of course we are talking about Gogol here. That guy messes up more than anyone I know."

"Rubi!" Xela cried.

"Hey, I just call 'em like I see 'em. Add to that the wacky Arms Akimbo, and anything is possible."

"That settles it," Autonomou said. She'd finally stopped pacing. "You two take the Alleviator to the surface and see if they're up there."

"Aye, aye, Captain," I said, giving Autonomou a salute.

"And hurry up. All this worrying is making me old before my time."

"Does she know she's already four hundred seventy-six?" I whispered to Xela as we left the lab by the back door.

"I heard that," shouted Dr. Autonomou.

13

"Just kidding!" Xela and I scurried down the back hall and stood in the center of the Alleviator room. Xela tilted her head back to look up the long shaft through the rock. My eyes followed hers. Well, her front two ones, anyway. Xela has a cool, prismlike eye in the back of her head. Always knows who's coming and going.

"That's a long way up," she said. "I'm always amazed to think that Dr. A built this herself."

"It's amazing, all right," I said. "But of course she was down here alone for two hundred years before we showed up." I pulled the flat, smooth, greenish disk that was the Alleviator key out of my pocket and pressed it. Suddenly a puff of air formed under our feet, lifting us up slightly.

"Next stop, Roma Gardens Park," the computer announced politely. "Please keep your arms and feet inside the ride at all times."

"I think we know that by now, computer," I said as we began to rise.

"Have a nice day," the computer chirped. In the next moment, we were shooting up the shaft at ya-hoo-yippee-ya-hoo speed. Standing on a puff of ultradense air is like standing on a big pillow. Except you can see a pillow. In this thing, it's like you're levitating. Fast.

"I can't look down in this thing," Xela said. "It's way too perpendicular."

"We're almost there," I said, as the crust bubble approached. That's always the part of the Alleviator ride I like best. Just when it looks like you're about to crash into the roof of the shaft, the thing slows way down and you pass right through the dirt as if it weren't there. And then, ta-da, you're above ground. Like walking through a cloud.

"Rubi!" Xela gasped, as we broke through to the surface. Totally panicked.

"What?" I asked. Then I saw. "Uh-oh, this could be trouble." The park all around us was swarming with students. They were all shapes. All sizes. All colors. It seemed like someone from every planet in the P.U. had shown up. And everyone was hooting, squishing, squirgaling. . . .

"What's going on?" Xela asked, standing perfectly still. "This place is always deserted. No one ever comes here. You can't very well have a secret entrance if it's in the middle of something."

"No kidding," I said. "Act casual. Maybe no one noticed that we just popped up out of nowhere."

"Actually," rasped a voice behind me, "consider yourselves noticed."

"She-Rak!" Xela exclaimed without turning around. "Am I glad to see you!"

"You are?" She-Rak and I said together. She-Rak was one of our classmates. If you liked tadpoles with spiked hair that spit out their food and spread it on their skin, you'd probably think he was fine. Actually, we found him something of a pain. A nice pain. But a pain. Especially since he'd followed Gogol into Autonomou's lab and learned about our secret missions. Now he *really* wanted to be one of us. But the vote was, four to zero, "No way!"

15

Xela turned around to look at She-Rak with her two front eyes. "Sure I'm glad to see you. You can tell us what's going on."

"Oh this? Guess it's my fault, really."

"You led all these life-forms over to the secret entrance to the lab? How could you! You know what'll happen if Autonomou is discovered."

"I know, I know. That's why I was standing here. To keep them away. How was I supposed to know they'd get so excited about harvest time?"

"Harvest time?" Xela asked. For the first time I noticed that some of the students were up in the bazookia trees, pulling pink blobby things off the limbs and tossing them to life-forms below.

"Yeah. We were all standing around the spaceport, waiting for our transports home, when Cho mentioned he was going home to planet Bupple to harvest the fruit off bazookia trees."

"Fruit?"

"Yeah. Big, squishy, sickeningly sweet chewy stuff. So I mentioned this hidden grove. It's the only place on Roma that has bazookia trees, you know."

"No, I didn't know that," I said dryly.

"And since we had time to waste . . ."

"Everyone just had to come here to try the fruit," Xela said. We looked out into the park. Life-forms were pulling, tugging, and tossing the pink blobs around.

She-Rak laughed. "It's fun. You tug on the stuff till it softens, then stick a whole bunch in your mouth, chew it, and blow huge, gigantic bubbles."

16

"Except there's one little problem," I said. "We could have been spotted popping out of the ground. Then the secret entrance would no longer be a secret and—"

"I'm sorry, Rubi, I didn't mean to—" *Splat!* A big glob of pink stuff hit She-Rak in the head. "Hey, cut that out, you dork-us!" She-Rak laughed, peeling the sticky stuff off his face. "See? Isn't this cool? It's all frubbery. And tasty, too." She-Rak opened his huge mouth. It was packed with the stuff. Then, in typical bottom-feeder fashion, he reached in with his hand, pulled the gooey, drippy mess out, and started smearing it on his stomach. Not a pretty sight. But, hey, he couldn't help it. That's how his species digests their food. "Want some?" He grinned. "Nice and soft."

Xela went from blue to green. "No thanks, She-Rak. Maybe some other time. We came to find Arms and Gogol. Have you seen them?"

"No, haven't seen them all day," he mumbled with his mouth full. "Why? Are you going on another mission?"

"She-Rak! Shhh!" I warned. "Not so loud. No, we're not going on any more missions. And if we were, we wouldn't tell you. So just forget about it."

"Gee, I was just asking."

"Rubi, we better get back to the lab," Xela said. "She-Rak, can you create a diversion?"

"Are you kidding?" She-Rak said. "It's what I do best! AAARRGGHHH!" he screamed, as he charged into the crowd, slinging half-chewed bazookia wads at everyone. I pushed the Alleviator key, and Xela and I were quickly lowered through the crust bubble.

"Now what?" Xela said, as we rode the puff of air to the bottom of the shaft.

"Now we worry." I sighed. Fortunately, we only had to waste about a nanomoment on that. Arms and Gogol were in the lab when we got back. And so was Dandoo, the Grand DOO-DUH.

He was the head of DUH. The Decidedly Officious Official of Diplomatic Universal Headquarters. Big title, but fitting for one of the most important life-forms in the P.U., and, as Autonomou's secret protector, the only other life-form in the universe who knew what was going on in this lab. Which was lucky for us. He'd already saved us more than once from the clutches of Professor Hal E. Toesis, who for some scary and very dark reason seemed to have it in for Dr. A. And all of us.

"Looks like the party started without us." I smiled. "Hello, Grand DOO-DUH, a pleasure to see you as always."

"Cut the charm, Rubi," Autonomou interrupted. Her eyeballs looked like they might pop out of their stalks. "Tell us what took you two so long."

"We ran into She-Rak and about a thousand of his friends," I said.

Xela looked at Arms and Gogol. "What I want to know is, where were you two?"

Arms rolled her eyes toward Dandoo and whispered,

18

"Gogol decided to take the long way, and I followed him."

"The Tunnels again," said Dandoo officially. "I'm sure I don't have to remind you they're strictly off-limits to all students."

"I'm sorry, sir," said Gogol. "I just needed time to be by myself. It was the only place I could think of."

"I'll let it go this time," said Dandoo, "but only because I'm concerned about you. I know the trial was rough. I came to the lab to say good-bye and see how you're doing."

Gogol shrugged. "Okay."

"I hope you're going to use this time off to relax," said Dandoo.

"Oh, no." Arms jumped in. "I'm going to Alzor with Gogol. And we've got all kinds of plans. Gogol's determined to finally find out—"

"What it would be like to pitch for the Lounge Lizards," interrupted Gogol as he pinched Arms's lower right arm. "They're playing the Sun Worshippers in the All-Alzorian Games. It's a dream of mine to hang out and tan with them."

"Really?" said Dandoo, raising a feathered brow.

"Absolutely," said Gogol.

"Listen, gang," said Xela as she circled the room, giving each of us an Earthling-type hug. "Hate to break this up, but I've got to be going. The space roamer for Numi leaves soon. I don't want to miss it. My family's giving me a welcome-home party. All three hundred and sixty-three of my brothers and sisters will be there."

19

"And by this time tomorrow, I'll be doing the bop on Douxwhop," I said with a smile.

"Well, while you are all off on your BATH," said Autonomou, "I'm going to stay here and make some improvements to this old computer system." Everyone groaned. Dr. A was brilliant, but sometimes her "improvements" did more harm than good.

"Think we can chance taking the Alleviator back up?" Xela asked.

"All space roamers are leaving Roma very shortly," said Dandoo. "I imagine everyone who was there before has headed for the spaceport by now."

The four of us made our way down the hall of the lab toward the Alleviator shaft. "Bye, Dr. A! Bye, Grand DOO-DUH!" yelled Arms as we entered the shaft. "Have a nice relaxing BATH!"

4

Arms Akimbo

Gogol and I piled into the space roamer to Alzor along with a bunch of other Alzorians and visitors headed for the reptile planet. I would have rather taken a Spaceway Gate and gone by wormhole, but space roamers were nearly as fast. Interplanetary wormhole travel was supposed to be reserved for important trips. Like secret missions to Earth.

"Welcome aboard, life-forms. This is your captain, Ow-tow, speaking. The good news is that if you're headed for Alzor you're on the right roamer. The bad news is that if Alzor is not your destination, it's too late. We're almost there!"

"Boy, that didn't take long," I said. "I didn't even have time to get a bag of Chortles."

"Look!" Gogol shouted, leaning over me to look out the window. "I'm home! That's Mount Opticus!"

"Oooh," I said. "It really does look like an eye. And, Gogol, it's following us."

"Just looks that way, Arms. And here comes Zrom Droma, the capital of Alzor."

"Wow." I gasped. "It's even prettier than in pictures!" The city was made up of gazillions of low-lying, pale pastel buildings with flat roofs and wide overhangs. "What's with the flat roofs?"

"As you know, Alzorians are reptiles. They like to lie out in the sun on the roofs. Then they use the shade below the overhangs if they get too hot."

"And the pointy things?" Every building had a tall, pointed spire decorated with colorful tiles that reached up hundreds of feet in the air. It was like looking at a forest of kaleidoscope trees.

"Ages ago they were used as lightning rods. Alzor used to have so many electrical storms that every building had to have one."

"How come 'used to'?"

"Once we joined the Planetary Union, scientists from planet Penx showed us how to eliminate electrical storms. The towers became useless. But everyone liked them so much, instead of tearing them down they decorated them. Even new buildings have them."

"Cool!"

22

"You should see them all lit up on holidays. Really something," Gogol said wistfully.

"Those of you with Homing Beacon Service should now gather at the rear of the roamer."

"Let's go, Arms."

"What are we doing?"

"Jumping out of the roamer."

"*What?*"

"Sure. You'll see, it's easy."

"It's not the jumping I'm worried about," I said as Gogol led me down the aisle. "It's the landing."

Gogol laughed. "Look, it's nothing. We get into disposable descent P-pods, my parents send out a homing beacon, and we float to their front door."

A smiling reptile greeted us at the back of the roamer. "Hope you don't mind, but there's a shortage of P-pods on board this roamer. More holiday traffic than we expected. The two of you will have to take one pod."

"But—" Gogol began to protest.

"No choice," the attendant said, holding open what looked like a giant beach ball. "Hop in or you'll miss your exit."

"Sounds good to me!" I said, heading back to my seat.

"No, come on, Arms," Gogol said, grabbing my sleeve. "You'll like it. I promise. It's very smooth and calming." Gogol slid into the flimsy ball first and leaned against the side. I followed him. As soon as I was in, the attendant snapped the entrance shut.

"Look at us, Gogol," I said. "Two P's in a pod."

"Now, just sit still and the stabilizers will keep you upright as you float to the surface," the attendant said. "Ready?"

"Sure," Gogol said.

"WAIT!" I screamed.

"What is it?" asked the attendant. I could see her through one of the clear panels.

"What if I don't sit still?"

"Then you'll spin wildly. Have a nice trip." She smiled, then pressed a button, and we began moving down a track. Gogol and I sat across from each other, our faces only inches apart. I spread my four arms out and found handholds along the walls.

Gogol laughed, "Don't worry, Arms. It's perfectly safe. You won't need to hold on."

I gave him a sly smile. "I'm holding on," I began as we reached the end of the track, "so I can rock this thing!" There was a small bump as we were tossed out the door of the space roamer and began falling—a nice, smooth, slow fall—toward the ground. That's when I began pulling this way and that, shifting my weight with each tug.

"No, Arms! NO!" yelled Gogol as I got the thing to begin to sway and pitch.

"You didn't really think I was scared, did you? Yee-hah! Whee!" I screamed. "We don't have anything like this on Armagettem! Whoa, whoa WAAAAAAAA!!!" Suddenly our slow, smooth fall got faster and faster. The pod began to spin, whirling in tighter and tighter circles.

Gogol didn't say much, but I think he was having fun. Finally, our pod bounced down with a hard bump. Instantly, the thing opened up. Standing right in front of us was an Alzorian life-form.

"Great greet!" it said.

"Mommy!" Gogol shouted. He tried to leap up and give her a hug, but for some reason his legs wouldn't work right. Mommy helped him from the pod while I crawled out using all four hands. As soon as I did, the pod folded itself into an envelope and mailed itself back to the roamer.

Once I was up on two feet, I couldn't stop staring at Gogol and his mother. I know it's rude, but I couldn't help it. I mean, he'd told us he was different from every other Alzorian and, of course, I'd met others. But standing there with his mother the difference was amazing. Gogol looked, well, okay, *nothing* like her. His mom was your basic two-legged, long-fingered, web-footed, scaly-skinned, long-snouted lizard lady. And Gogol was, well, almost a perfect Earthling-like human.

"Great greet," another life-form called as it approached. "I'm Gogol's dad, Renza."

"And I'm Arms Akimbo," I said.

"Of course you are, dear," Gogol's dad said. "But don't you worry. Those arms will come in useful one day."

"But I—"

"Hi, dad," Gogol said with a smile. "How are you?"

"Great-great as always. Listen, Gogol. Dinner's almost ready. Why don't you show your friend around

25

the farm for a bit? Then come in and tell us all about how everything is going at DUH.''

"Okay," Gogol said. His parents hissed and loped off to the house. "Come on, Arms."

We walked past the low, flat house and down a wide lane. "So this is where you grew up?" I asked. For the first time since we landed, I got a chance to take a look around. Alzor's pale green sky was clear of any clouds. A big, white sun hung high above us. Not many other houses, either. Gogol's farm was way out in the sticks. Literally. Fields of purple, waist-high stick things were growing everywhere.

"That's the main crop, wheetle. Alzorians make everything from it. Food, clothes, glue . . .''

"Sounds yummy."

"The stuff grows like a weed. We don't even harvest it anymore."

"Then who are all those life-forms working in the fields?"

"Tourists."

"Huh?"

"The Alzorian government has plenty of wheetle, so they pay my parents *not* to grow it. Instead, stressed-out city-dwellers from all over the Planetary Union come here to work on their vacations. It's supposed to help them relax and get back in touch with nature. We call them jolly ranchers, give them brightly colored costumes to wear, and treat them like dirt. They love it."

26

"Gee, that sounds so . . . jolly," I said, not really meaning it. "So what do they do all day?"

"Pretend they're farmers, raise protein bugs, grow leafy things, build fences . . ."

"Out of the way!!" a voice screamed from behind us. Gogol grabbed my lower left arm and pulled me to the side of the road just as a huge Trakter glided by.

"Hey, watch it!" Gogol yelled.

"How do you stop this thing?" the driver—if you could call him that—asked. Before Gogol could answer, the jolly guy ran through a fence, over a pile of boxes, and into a ditch. Guess that's why they call them ranchers.

"Push the red button!" Gogol yelled. The machine squealed to a stop. "Amateurs," Gogol muttered under his breath.

"Guess repairing fences will be tomorrow's fun activity!"

"It won't be the first time." Gogol laughed. "We put that fence there for a reason. Gives them something to do."

The sound of a hitsu chiming got our attention. "Great goo-time!" Gogol's mom called. "Yoo-hoo! Goo-gol. Arrrmss!"

"Dinner time!"

"Will we be eating with all these cheery tourists?"

"Nope. Just you, me, Mom, and Dad. One big happy family."

"Really? I wouldn't call that big. I mean, Xela has three hundred and sixty-three brothers and sisters. Now, that's big. You're just an only child. Which seems to me to be pretty little and—"

"Arms?" Gogol interrupted. "Put a sock in it."

"Ooooh. Is that what you eat on this planet? Wish I'd bought that bag of Chortles."

5

Gogol

"So, Gogolly," my dad said in that annoying singsong way of his.

I winced. "I wish you wouldn't call me that."

"Is going to school at DUH everything you hoped it would be?"

"We see you're getting wonderful grades," Mom added, "but has it been okay?"

"Actually, yes," I said. "I've made some really good friends. Arms is one of the best."

"That's right! If it weren't for me, Gogol would still be a lonely, sad know-it-all," Arms teased.

Dad looked shocked. "You mean you're not a know-it-all, Gogol?"

"Sure I am, Dad. Arms was just kidding around." Alzorians are not known for their sense of humor, and my mom and dad were no exception.

"I'm a kidder," Arms said with a smile.

"Oh, I see," Dad said dryly. "Care for some borscht?"

"Umm . . . what is it?"

"Why, it's a sort of beet soup, dear," Mom said, scooping a huge spoonful into a dish.

"What's a beet? Sounds violent."

"No, it's a vegetable actually. They only grow here on our farm for some reason."

"The borscht is from an ancient family recipe," Dad added. "No one seems to know where it came from."

"Just like me," I said.

"Gogolly, you just got here. Please don't start on that again," said Dad.

"I can't help it. I can't stop thinking about it. It's so easy for you and Mom. You know who you are. You fit in. I'm a freak. And I've *got* to know why."

"Not tonight, Gogol," boomed my father.

"We're so happy to have you home, dear," added my mother. "Let's just have a nice happy family meal." Like it or not, the subject was closed. The Code of Values forbids disrespecting your parents, so somehow or other, I was going to have to sit there eating my borscht and pretending everything was okay. Even while I could feel my blood begin to boil.

"I have a few questions I'd like to ask," I suddenly heard Arms pipe up.

"About Alzor?" my father asked with a big relieved smile.

"Well, actually, about Gogol." Whew, this was going to be interesting. It's also against the Code of Values to disrespect a guest. I knew I should have shut Arms down, but I was too desperate to hear my parents' answers. And, besides, she had that look in her eye that told me it was no use trying to stop her. So I didn't. "Now, why did you move to this farm after Gogol was born?"

Mom looked at me with a weary expression. "Do you really want to go through this all again, Gogol?"

"It's not up to me, Mom. She's the guest." Then she looked at my father. He just slowly nodded his head.

"All right," she said. "You win, Gogol." Then she turned toward Arms. "This farm had always been in my family. For generations. But when I met Gogol's father at the university we decided to settle in the capital so we could pursue our careers as scientists. Gogol's grandparents were still alive then. Still running the farm. So it wasn't a problem."

Dad took over. "Then we had Gogol. And as he's forever reminding us, he looked so different from any other life-form that many considered him to be—"

"Unsightly? Ugly? Despicable? Vile? A little homely?" offered Arms.

"ARMS!" I screamed.

31

"Just trying to get to the bottom of all this, Gogol. No offense."

"Yes, Arms," Dad said. "I'm sorry to say you're right. Others would stare, tease, and make fun of him. So we thought it best to move back to the farm in order to protect him. To try to give him a chance at a normal upbringing."

"Normal?" Arms laughed. "We must not be talking about the same Gogol." Then she loudly slurped the soup. "Mmm-mmm good. If you write down the recipe, I'll try to get it to my friends, the Campbells, in Scotland."

"Huh?" said my mom.

"Oops," Arms said. "Never mind. It's a long story. So why does Gogol look this way in the first place?" She reached over and squeezed my cheeks with her top two hands.

"Ow! Cut it out." I groaned.

"That's a good question, Arms," Mom said. "We always assumed it was just the result of a random muta- tion in his DN-Aydoh."

"What did the doctors say?" asked Arms.

Mom and Dad both looked down. They were quiet for a few moments. Then, Mom explained. "We never took him to a doctor, Arms. We were afraid they'd want to take him away from us."

"We couldn't let that happen. No matter what, he's our son," Dad said. He gave me a smile. I smiled back.

"Hey, maybe he was switched at birth."

"ARMS!" I felt like she was taking this a little too far.

"Just a thought!"

"We thought about that, of course," Mom said. "But his father sat on the egg for weeks and weeks until it hatched."

"I never got up off that blasted thing. Not even to eat!"

"Thanks, Dad," I said.

"You were late hatching, too."

"I know. You've told me."

"Have I?" Dad asked. *Only about a million times,* I thought.

"But I still don't see—" Arms began.

Mom jumped in before Arms could ask another question. "That's all we can tell you about this, Arms."

"Because that's all we know," Dad added with finality.

I had to speak up. "Lately, I've been having some weird dreams. More like visions really."

My parents suddenly looked a little nervous. "What kind of visions, dear?" Mom asked evenly.

"Arms was with me at the time. I kind of saw myself sitting on top of a tall, tall rocket and blasting off from a strange, primitive world."

"True. That's what he told me," Arms said.

"And then, I felt like I was trapped in a closet and frozen solid. Then, Alzor came into view, but like it was a long time ago. And some letters, C-C-C-P, kept floating by. What do you make of that?"

33

"It was a fantasy, Gogol. Nothing more," Dad tried to assure me.

"I don't think so. It was so real. I think maybe I tapped into ancient images set in my DN-Aydoh. You know, like from the collective memory."

"Tapping into the Alzorian collective memory is a rare talent, Gogol," Mom said, getting up from the table. "And you don't have it. Trust me."

"Your mother's right," Dad added. "You probably just had gas. What did you have to eat that day?"

"It wasn't gas, Dad."

"Good! Well, that's settled then. Why don't you show Arms to the guest room. I'm sure she's tired after such a long day."

"No, actually," Arms started to say.

"Sure she is," I said, glad to have a reason to leave the trough. "Come on, Arms."

"All right. Good night, you two," my folks said together as we went down the hall.

Arms leaned over and whispered in my ear. "Gogol, I get the feeling your parents know a lot more than they pretend not to know."

"No kidding," I said. "Go ahead and turn around. What do you see?"

Arms looked back and gasped. "Your parents are watching us. Staring. Not moving at all. Like they're frozen."

"It's a lizard thing. They get motionless if they're threatened or scared."

"Gogol," Arms said nervously, "what's going on?"

"That's what I hope you'll help me find out, Arms. I grew up with this."

"Wow."

"Here's your room," I said, pulling back the draped door. "Will this be okay?"

Arms smiled as she walked around the nest. She crouched down and felt the wheetle-stuffed pillows. Then she went to the side table and held up a large clear container filled with buzzing protein bugs.

"The bed is great, but what's this?"

"Oh, I guess you won't be needing that," I said, taking it from her. "It's a snack holder in case you get hungry in the middle of the night."

"Do you eat bugs, too, Gogol?"

"No, not *live* anyway. I only like them in the borscht."

Arms pale orange skin blanched. "There were bugs in the borscht?"

"I figured it was best you didn't know."

"You were right," she said as her knees gave way and she collapsed into the nest. "OOooohhh! I don't feel so good."

"See you in the morning!" I said, cheerfully pulling the drape closed behind me.

"Don't be so sure!" Arms moaned.

6

Gogol

"Gogol, if you don't mind, I'd like to skip breakfast," Arms said. She still looked a little pale.

"Suits me. We can get an earlier start." Arms followed me down the hall that led to the living area. Dad was busying himself in the kitchen. "I'm going to show Arms the sights downtown, Dad. We'll grab something to eat there."

"Are you sure?" he asked. "I was just about to pour some reheated borscht over a bowl of boiled Wheetley's."

Arms turned away and swallowed hard. "No, thanks. Really."

"Where's Mom?" I asked.

"Out sunning herself," Dad replied. "Be home for dinner?"

Arms smiled. "Can I ask what we're having?"

"Of course. A meal from the garden. Baked leafy ratatat-spitooee."

Arms looked at me. "No bugs," I whispered.

"Count us in!" she said. Then the two of us headed downtown.

Arms and I took the Express Belt right to the heart of Zrom Droma. It was Arms's first time to ride it and I was worried she'd be nervous, which would be totally understandable. The belt whizzes by at P-force speed, packed with life-forms. But they're just a blur because the belt never stops. To get on, you're lifted in the air and moved down the track at the same speed as the belt. Then, when there's an opening, the system sets you down. "Arms?" I said as we went barreling down the track. "Are you okay?"

"Whee!!" was all she said.

"So you like it."

"It's even better than the Arms Twister on Armagettem. I could ride this all day!"

"Sorry, but we're getting off at the next stop."

"Already?" Arms said sadly. The Express Belt exit module lifted us out of our seats and set us off to the side.

"Here we are," I said. "Downtown Zrom Droma."

"So I take it we're not here to tour the monuments, right?" Arms asked as we approached a large structure.

"Right," I said. "This is where we start digging for

37

facts." We looked up at the entrance to an impressive building. A motto was carved in stone above the door.
KNOWLEDGE IS FREE. TAKE SOME. SHARE SOME.

"Where are we?"

"This is the main BRAIN building. Home of the Big Reptile for All Information Needs."

"You mean like a Holographic Information Tub?"

"Not really. A HIT unit is a computer. The BRAIN is a life-form."

Arms thought about that as we entered the lobby. "And what exactly are you looking for, Gogol?"

"I figure that one of my ancient ancestors must have married an Earthling. So I want to find out if Alzorians have ever visited Earth."

"Makes sense," Arms agreed.

"May I help you?" hissed a narrow-faced creature standing at a tall desk.

"I'd like to see the BRAIN," I said.

The desk clerk looked at me intensely. "This facility is only for Alzorians," he said.

I placed my right hand on the Recognizer and peeled my collar down so he could see the back of my neck. "I *am* Alzorian," I declared. "See?"

"Ah. Yes, I see," he said. "Well, you must have an appointment."

"I do. The name is Gogol. Check your list." I watched as the desk lizard reviewed the information in front of him.

"And what is your business?" he asked without looking up.

38

"We want to find out about Earth," Arms blurted out.

"Earth?" the clerk spat out. "Never heard of it."

"I'm sorry. I must have missed something. Are *you* the BRAIN?" I asked impatiently. No response. "Listen, please. I'm here on very important business. May we see the BRAIN now?"

"Wait here."

"Geez," exclaimed Arms. "Not too friendly. Is this the only way to find stuff on Alzor?"

"No, I just figured I'd start at the top." Suddenly the desk lizard reappeared.

"The BRAIN will see you now," he said matter-of-factly. "You have seventeen point three seconds."

"Gosh, thanks," I said. A large door opened behind the desk. Arms and I went through into a round chamber.

"Whoa!" Arms whispered. "Look at that guy." In front of us stood the BRAIN, a beautiful, multicolored, frilled lizard with a huge head and a feathered hat. Tubes ran from the hat to an array of crystal computers. A kaleidoscope of lights rotated across the walls and ceiling. The BRAIN's frill vibrated and filled our hearing ports with a humming sound.

"Planet RU1:2," he said in a shrill, trancelike voice. "Also known as Earth. Third planet in a Class Seven solar system located in the thirty-seventh quadrant on the fringe of the known universe. Densely populated by semi-intelligent life-forms. Self-destructive. Unworthy of membership in the Planetary Union. All travel

39

banned. Estimate the planet's resources will be exhausted and ecosystem will collapse in one quardnip of time. End of file."

"That's *it?*" I said, shocked.

"That is all the accessible data. End of file," the BRAIN repeated. The colored lights in the room dimmed.

"Come on," I pleaded. "There *must* be more. Something about a mission to Earth? Visitations?"

"Gogol," Arms said gently, "maybe that really is it."

"No, Arms, I know there's more." I turned to face the BRAIN. "You are supposed to be the biggest know-it-all of all. Why won't you tell me more? What are you hiding?"

"Time's up," the desk lizard called from the door.

"Wait, I need to know—"

"Come on, Gogol, let's go," Arms said, leading me to the exit.

The fresh air felt good. I sat down on a ledge outside the building. "Blew it, didn't I?"

Arms threw an arm over my shoulder. "Let's just say that insulting the main BRAIN probably wasn't the best thing you could have done."

"I just know he knew more than he would say, Arms."

"So why wouldn't he tell you? Why would he want to hide stuff from you?"

"That's what we have to find out," I said, sucking

40

in a huge gulp of air and standing up. "Let's get going. Next, we'll visit the Lobes."

"The Lobes?"

"Right, they're scattered all over town. Areas of the BRAIN system with specialized knowledge. Maybe we can get bits and pieces of information from them."

"Whatever," Arms said. "I'm just along for the ride."

The Frontal Lobe was just past the Tower Terrace, not far from the BRAIN building. We checked in at the desk and were shown to the area with all the volumes of information about travel to other planets. But something was wrong.

"When I chose Volume E on the screen nothing came, Gogol," Arms said as she quickly ran through the reference files.

"There is no Volume E," the lobe librarian explained. She was standing right behind Arms.

"How could that be? We're looking for information about Earth. Earth starts with an 'E'. I'm sure other things start with 'E' too."

The librarian let out a huge sigh. "Just a moment," she said looking at her own computer display. "Oh, I see. Volume E is being serviced. Try in three weeks."

"That won't do," I said. "I need the information now."

"Gogol!" Arms said in a sudden, desperate whisper.

"What?"

"That blue lizard guy over there. I think he's watching us."

"Where?" I said, looking around.

"Standing against the blue wall, in a blue trench coat. He's the exact same color as the wall."

I followed her gaze until I found him. "He's a chameleon. They blend into whatever they stand in front of. But why would he be watching us, Arms?"

"I don't know, but he is. And I say we do something about it."

"Okay, okay," I said to indulge her. "We're on our way to the other side of town. If he follows us all the way to the Lower Lobe, we'll know for sure he's after us."

"Sure wish Xela were here to keep an eye out for him," said Arms as we entered the Express Belt.

"Yeah," I agreed. "An eye in the back of your head does come in handy." Arms held up all four of her arms and waved her hands in the air.

"These come in handy," she corrected me. "An eye in the back of your head comes in . . . comes in . . . eyes-ically. Yeah. That's the word. Eyes-ically. Like it?"

"Brilliant." I smiled.

"Thank you," said Arms. "I do my best."

"I know," I said. "And guess what? While you were being brilliant, we reached our exit." We de-boarded and went straight to the Lower Lobe. Arms wasted no time heading for the large HIT unit.

Seconds later, she called out, "Gogol, I think I found something!" Suddenly, in front of her, a rotating three-dimensional holographic model of Earth appeared.

"Way to go, Arms," I shouted, running over to her. "See if you can find anything about Alzorian contact with Earth."

42

"Okay, I . . . uh-oh," she said as the hologram disappeared.

"What happened?"

"Dear visitors," a computer voice announced, "the Lower Lobe is experiencing an unexpected power failure. Please exit immediately."

"This is very weird, Gogol," Arms said as we filed out. "I'm beginning to think something's going on here. Something that goes way beyond your looking like an Earthling."

"I know what you mean, Arms."

"Good. So you'll stop asking questions now?"

"Are you kidding? I'm more interested than ever!"

Arms moaned. "That's what I was afraid of." Then, suddenly, she blurted out, "Whoa! Did you see that?"

"What?"

Arms shook her head. "Gogol, as soon as we got outside, a creature darted around the corner."

"So? That's what lizards do. They dart."

"I'm telling you, we're being watched."

"Look, it's late and we're both getting tired. Let's try just one more place, then head home."

"Where now?" asked Arms wearily.

"The BRAIN Stem," I replied. "The information there is pretty basic, but sometimes it's helpful."

"Earth?" The BRAIN Stem worker said through the narrow window. "Yes, we have some information on Earth. What do you want to know?"

43

"I want to know about any ancient missions that Alzor may have conducted to Earth."

"There were none."

"There's never been *any* contact between Earthlings and Alzorians?"

"No. Good-bye."

"Wait! How can you be so sure?"

"Mr. Gogol . . ." the worker began.

A chill ran down my spine. "You know my name?"

"Of course. I was told to expect you," she said. The panic I felt inside must have been visible on my face, because all of a sudden the worker's face softened. Dropping her voice to barely a whisper she said, "Trust me on this, and I say this as a friend, you're better off not asking these questions. You've raised the concern of some very powerful reptiles."

"But, I—"

"That's all I can say!" She quickly slammed the window opening shut.

"Gogol, look!" Arms shouted, pointing. "It's that guy again. But now he's orange!"

"The chameleon!" I said. "I guess you're right, Arms. He must be part of all this." I headed straight for him.

"Gogol, stop! What are you doing?"

"I have to find out what's going on, Arms." As I charged up to the chameleon, he froze. "All right, you. Why are you following us?"

"And don't even think of trying any funny stuff," Arms said, running up to join me. "I'm an expert in

44

hand-to-hand sport-dancing! Ha! Ho! Heh!'' Both the chameleon and I stood back and watched as Arms sliced and kicked through the air with all six appendages.

"Arms," I said. "It's okay."

"Whaa-hoo! Yah, wah, whoo!"

The chameleon shivered and said, "Your friend is ssscaring me."

"Knock it off, Arms!"

"Oops. Guess I got carried away. Sorry, sorry!"

The chameleon relaxed. He looked at me and began to hiss. "Messsssage for you, Missster Gogol. My employer hasss information you may find valuable."

"Who is it?" I said urgently. "Who is your employer?"

"Can't ssay. Meet tonight. Encrusted Cavernss. Sssecond chamber passs the Cryssstal Pool. S'sactly halfway to dawn."

"How will I know it's him?"

"You'll know. Sss'all I can ssay. Oh, isss one thing more," he said, holding out a webbed hand. "S'spare ssome fliess?"

"Sorry," I said. "I'm fresh out." The chameleon looked disappointed. He dropped to all fours and scampered away.

"Gee," said Arms, "meeting a mysterious life-form in the tunnels at midnight? Sounds like we're back on good old Roma!"

"I don't like it, Arms."

"Why not? You may have finally found someone willing to help you."

"Could be," I said as we began to head home. "Or . . ."

"Or," gasped Arms as she completed my thought, "it could be a trap!"

7

Arms Akimbo

"So tell us all about your day," Dad asked, as he pulled a stool up to the dinner trough. "What sights did you see?"

I didn't know what to say. We'd spent the whole time talking to brains and brain parts. So I dropped them a Rubi—my most dazzling smile—and said, "We went to Zrom Droma. It's very, um . . . busy."

"Busy, yes," Gogol's mom noted. "But did Gogol show you the Spire of Spare? The Outer Obstacles? Did you ride to the top of Mount Opticus?"

"I wanted to, but—"

Gogol jumped in. "We didn't want to do everything in one day, Mom. Arms will be with us for a while."

"That's true," his mother agreed. "But you must have some impression of our planet, Arms."

"Um . . . well . . . it all went by kind of like a blur. I said, 'Whee!' Gogol thought I'd like it. Then we walked by some tall buildings. Everything seemed very smart. And colorful. Frillery, really. And I really liked the way some lizards, oops, excuse me, I mean some Alzorians matched the background. It was cool." Gogol's parents smiled at me politely, then looked at him kind of helplessly.

"You asked," Gogol said, I thought a little too apologetically.

"So how *did* you spend your time, Son?" asked Gogol's dad.

"We mainly just went to the library."

"Good-great! That's very studious of you," Gogol's dad said. "Why?"

"Homework," I said. "I'm doing a report on how I spent my Break-Away-To-Home vacation and I needed to do some research."

"They certainly work you hard at DUH," he said.

"Yep, they do," I said, taking a big bite of stuff. "By the way, the food is great tonight. I like this non-buggy stuff."

"Hey, do like I do," Gogol's mother said, rattling a jar. "Sprinkle dried bugs on top. Gives a nice crunch."

UGH! "I'll pass, thanks." I smiled.

After dinner, Gogol and I played a game of Snar-

48

peesy with his folks. It was kind of fun, but sort of gross. I liked the part where you tried to get your bug to race around a board. But I had to look away whenever Gogol's Mom or Dad shot out their tongues to keep the bugs on track. At the end of the game they offered to let me eat my bug as a special treat. Gogol took pity on me and told his parents I was exhausted and better get to bed.

"Next time," I said as I backed out down the hall.

"Okay," said Gogol's mom reassuringly. "We'll save a nice big juicy one for you."

As soon as we were out of sight, Gogol led me silently out the back door and to another building. There, he pulled out a small, two-seated transport.

"Come on, Arms. We'll ride my old IF scooter to the tunnels."

"IF scooter?" I said, eyeing the thing. It had no wheels of any kind and seemed to just hang in the air.

"IF stands for 'It Floats,' " Gogol explained. "It's just your basic antigravity vehicle. Hop on. We need to hurry."

Even though the sun was down, our way was lit by a pale blue light. The Alzor sky never really went black. Instead, it glowed with a kind of electric blue light that flashed and surged all night long. "It's the falsphurs in the atmosphere that are excited by gravity waves," Gogol explained. "It happens in the daytime too, but you can't see it."

I didn't really care why it happened. It was beautiful. I leaned back, watched the sky, and tried to imagine

49

how cool it would be to grow up on a planet where every night was a laser light show.

"You're really lucky to have grown up here, Gogol."

"It's really no big deal. Like everything else, you get used to it." *Too bad,* I thought. I was so busy watching the sky show it seemed like only nanoseconds had passed before Gogol started slowing down to look for the entrance to the tunnels.

"Here we are," he said as he brought the IF to a stop. We climbed off and went inside the mountain. Gogol pulled out a light stick. Just one. "Don't you have one for me, too?" I asked, just a *little* whiny.

Gogol smiled. "You won't need one."

"Gee, thanks a lot," I said. "Leave your guest to pick her way through the shadows while you—" Then, Gogol held his light stick up. The place turned so bright, I had to put all four hands over my eyes. I peeked a little, but I couldn't see a thing. Finally, my eyes adjusted. "Roma-Rama!" I screamed.

"What is it? What's the matter?"

"This place. These tunnels. They're fantastic!"

Gogol looked around. "Yeah, I guess so."

"Are you kidding? When the chameleon said encrusted caverns, I thought he meant encrusted with slime and dreck and rotten stuff. Like Roma's tunnels. I had no idea he meant encrusted with jewels and sparkly metals and crystals and—"

"Look, Arms, I'm sorry but there's no time to sightsee. We have to hurry. It's almost time."

"But if you think this might be a trap, shouldn't we,

kind of, sort of check the place out? Come up with a plan? Not go off and do something *stupid?*"

"It might be dangerous, but I can't miss this chance. Stay here if you want. I'll be back soon."

"You hope." I sighed under my breath as I watched him disappear into the tunnels.

51

8

Arms Akimbo

"I'll stay here and watch his back," I said aloud to no one. Being backup was a good thing, I had decided. But as Gogol's light faded, I had another thought. Staying back now means being alone! In the dark!

Jumping up, I tore through the tunnel, yelling, "Gogol! Gogol!" It was what I'd call kind of a quiet yell. I didn't want to give our position away. As I entered a round cave with a crystal-clear pool of water in the middle, I heard Gogol hiss, "Sssshhh."

"Geez!" I cried. Quietly. "You scared me!"

"Be quiet, you'll wake them," said Gogol.

"Who or what are you talking about?"

Gogol pointed to the other side of the pool. "It's a colony of loquacious lounging lizards."

The creatures were sleeping on terraces of rock above the water. Each one was no bigger than my hand. "They're so little and cute!"

"No to mention, brilliant. Many become top scientists. They feed on the crystals down here. They say crystal power makes them smarter."

"Really?"

"Uh-huh. But please don't wake them. They've got opinions about everything." Then Gogol took my hand. "Arms, thanks for coming. It's just a little farther."

"Second chamber to the left," I said. "Right?"

"No. Left," Gogol stated.

I nodded in agreement. "Right."

"No, I'm sure he said left."

"Right! I'm agreeing with you!" I said again.

A voice I didn't recognize—high-pitched and with a strange accent—came out of nowhere. "Say what can be understood. If you agree with left, say 'correct.' "

"Correct!" I said, not wanting to upset the owner of the voice.

"Knowledge is free," croaked out a different voice.

"Take some!" sang another.

"Share some!" added a fourth.

"Uh-oh. We've woken up the loquacious loungers," I said.

"So you have," a voice said that sounded kind of eerie and nothing like the others. I whipped my head

53

around just in time to see a life-form come out of the shadows. It was dressed in a heavy woven robe that covered every bit of its body including its head.

I turned to Gogol and whispered, "I don't like this. Why all the mystery?"

"I don't know, Arms," he whispered, holding up his light stick. "Who are you?" The life-form turned its back to us.

"Help you, I will. Must not try to see my face. Agree, yes?" It wasn't said angrily. Just very matter-of-factly.

Gogol looked at me, lowered the light stick, and shrugged. I double-shrugged back. "Agreed," we answered.

"What's your name?" I asked.

"Yada-Yada," came the reply.

"What does that mean?"

"Anything you'd like," replied the mysterious stranger. "That's the beauty of it."

"Well, it's a little odd, but I can deal with that. It's not as bad as 'Wharteen-o-boffa-louee-chumpa-dingle.' A cute little life-form I know from the planet of Op, who—"

"Arms!" Gogol interrupted. "Could we get on with this, please? I'm sure Mr. Yada-Yada has other appointments to keep tonight."

"Wise boy, you are. Speaks truth," Yada-Yada said, his voice turning serious. "In danger, you two. Questions asked, feathers ruffled."

"But lizards don't have feathers," I said, trying to be helpful. Suddenly I felt Gogol's hand close over my mouth.

"I'm just trying to find out where I came from," he said. "Why should anyone else even care?"

54

"Mummumu . . . mumu," I tried to add from behind Gogol's hand. But the stranger just ignored me.

"Many care," he continued. "Lives may be in danger. Reputations at stake. Scandal. Disgrace!"

"Okay, okay! I get the idea," said Gogol, finally releasing me. He looked down for a long moment and sighed. "So you want me to give up, right?"

"Contrary! Help you, I will."

"I have an idea," I said. "Why don't you just tell Gogol what he wants to know."

As Gogol put his hand back over my mouth, the stranger answered, "Cannot do that. Wisdom unearned has no lasting value. You must find truth on your own." He moved over to a boulder and sat down. "Now, tell me what you know."

Gogol took a breath, let go of me, and started pacing. "Okay, I know that my DN-Aydoh is half-Earthling and half-Alzorian. I'm a mutant, and from what I can tell, the only one. There's no one else like me anywhere in the universe. On one of my trips to Earth, I learned that my name, Gogol, is a name given to life-forms in an area called Russia. I also—"

"Ha! Maybe should go there!" Yada-Yada suggested.

"Go to Russia? Well, I guess I could. But in what time period? What part? I need coordinates."

"Yada, yada."

"Excuse me?"

"You talk when you should listen," Yada-Yada said. He reached out and handed something to Gogol. "These are the coordinates you seek. Go to Earth. Answers lie there."

Gogol cradled the coordinates in both hands. His eyes got misty. I saw him shudder. "Thank you, Yada." Then the hooded stranger stepped back into the shadows and began to make his way down the tunnel. "Will I see you again?" Gogol cried after him.

"Time will tell, it will."

I ran to Gogol's side. He looked like he was in shock. "Are you okay?"

"Okay?" he said, breaking into a grin. "You bet I'm okay! In fact, I'm way better than okay. Do you know what this means?"

"I'm never going to get to sklii down Mount Opticus?"

"Arms, if Yada-Yada is right, these coordinates will lead me to the answer I've been looking for."

"Only one little problem," I said. "As far as I know, there's only one wormhole to Earth."

"Right, in Autonomou's lab. So?"

"So we have to make up some excuse to explain to your parents why we suddenly have to rush back to Roma, try to find Dr. A, who, for all we know might have gone fishing on planet Hookem, convince her to help us, and—"

"Arms?"

"And then get her old clunker of a computer back on-line, and—"

"Arms! It's okay. We can do it. Trust me." Then Gogol got very quiet. Taking two of my hands in his he asked, "Will you come with me?"

"Me? Abandon you? Never happen. I wouldn't miss this for all the bug borscht in the universe!"

9

Gogol

I drove the IF scooter at P-force speed across the fields of wheetle, headed for home.

"Going a little fast, aren't we?" Arms shouted over the wind noise. She actually sounded kind of nervous for a change. I backed off the speed a little.

"Sorry, Arms. I was lost in thought," I admitted. "I sure hope Dr. Autonomou is in the lab. It'll make things a whole lot easier if she helps us."

"No kidding. Otherwise, we'll have to wait until she gets back."

"Why? You can run her computer, Arms. I know

you can," I said. "I'll just have to go to Earth alone while you stay on the controls."

"Gogol, do you really think that's a good idea? First of all, I don't think Dr. A. would like us breaking and entering into her computer. *Again.* And secondly, you're going to need me on Earth."

"Agreed, but we can't wait, Arms. Remember what Yada-Yada said? Lives are at stake." We were both quiet for a little while. Then I asked, "What do you think he meant by that, Arms?"

"Could have meant that life-forms would die if you find the answers you're looking for."

I gasped. "You don't really think—"

"No, of course not," Arms answered. "I might think that if we were on Earth, but not here in the good old, peace-loving Planetary Union. I think he meant the careers of some public officials could be over. But, hey, if they're hiding some big, dark secret . . ."

"And apparently, they are," I said.

"Looks that way. Something that goes against the Code of Values. Big time."

"So we'd be doing the right thing if we helped expose them, right?"

"Abso-tootly, Gogol." Arms smiled. "We're doing the right thing."

"Okay." I sighed. "Thanks."

I got us back to the house just before sunrise. Well, it's not really a sun that rises, but we call it that anyway. Alzor is so far away from its sun that in order for this planet to be livable, scientists had to position gigantic lenses all through the solar system to concentrate light and heat in our direction. When all that energy reaches Alzor, it's bounced off a huge mirror that orbits the planet, warming everything up. It even looks like a sun, and serves the same purpose.

Knowing my parents would be up soon, I silently crept to my room and lay down. But I was too excited to sleep. I couldn't stop thinking about Earth and what I might find there. My mind started to drift. . . .

All of a sudden I felt as if I were weightless, floating in space. Below me was a bright blue planet. It was slowly turning. Peaceful and silent. Then, as I watched, some kind of spaceship came around from behind it and headed straight for me. The craft was small and round. As it got closer, I could see the letters C.C.C.P. on the side right next to a window. I drifted over and looked in. The walls were covered with switches and little lights. Three sleeping life-forms were crammed side by side. I looked closely at the one nearest me. I felt like I recognized the face.

"Gogol?" I heard a whispery voice say from very far away. Still, I stared at the face in the spacecraft. He looked *very* familiar, but I couldn't place him.

"Gogol?" I heard the voice whisper again, a little closer. I was sure I knew that face. I started to shake.

"GOGOL!" screamed the voice. *YES! The face was me!*

"Aaarrgghh!" I screamed, sitting up like a bolt of charged ions.

"Sorry, sorry!" the voice said. Arms Akimbo was

standing over me. "You were sleeping so soundly, I had to shake you awake."

"I was sleeping?" I asked through a haze of confusion.

"Yes, sorry. But I figured you'd want to get going."

I rubbed my eyes with both hands. "Arms, I had another vision. I saw—"

"The space rover for Roma is coming to pick you up soon, Son," I heard my dad say. "You better get ready."

"Arms told us all about your little project, dear," added Mom. They were standing in the doorway to my room.

"She did?" I looked at Arms for an explanation, but she looked away.

"Yes, she told us everything."

"ARMS!" I shouted. How could she!

"I thought they should know."

"We're very impressed with you, Gogol," Mom said in her sweetest voice.

"Wha . . . you are? You're not mad?"

"Why should we be mad?" Dad chuckled. "Not hardly. We think it was great-great of you to be so concerned about us. But don't worry, you and Arms go on back to Roma."

Mom nodded. "Then, as soon as you're done with your lab assignment—"

"Lab assignment?" I stood up next to Arms and gave her a questioning look.

"Sure, Gogol. Remember?" she explained. "Professor Yada? The assignment he gave us for extra credit

60

that you didn't want do to because it would interfere with your trip home, and . . ."

I finally woke up and realized what was going on. "Oh, *that* lab assignment. Gosh, Mom and Dad. Thanks for understanding."

"Of course," said my father. "But I'm curious, what do you have to do, exactly?"

Arms jumped back in. "First we have to translate some interstellar coordinates, solve the equations for warp-time travel, chart a wormhole course. Then, the real work begins."

Mom laughed as she ushered us out of the room. "Okay, okay! I think we get the idea. Come on, you'll be late for the space rover."

"Well, good luck," Dad said, as he zipped us into our ascent pods. "We'll keep some borscht on the boil for your return!"

"Gee, thanks." Arms smiled. It didn't take long for us to be drawn into the space rover and get settled into our seats. I looked over at Arms and gave her a sly grin. "Professor Yada?"

"I thought it was a nice touch," she said, shrugging all four shoulders.

"Arms," I said, "have I ever told you you're a genius?"

"Not lately."

"Well, you are. Thanks."

Arms smiled and turned to look out the window. Mount Opticus was fading into the distance. She stared as it went by. "Maybe next time," I heard her say.

61

10

Arms Akimbo

"We're home!" I yelled as Gogol and I flew out of the Alleviator and into Dr. A's lab. There she sat. Right where we'd left her. Fiddling with the computer.

"You're home, too!" cried Gogol, barely able to hide his relief. But the doctor didn't move. She didn't say hi back. She just went on doing what she'd been doing, acting like we weren't even there.

"We're home!" I said again. "Aren't you excited?" Finally, one of her eyes swung around in my direction.

"You've only been gone two days," she said.

"But we missed you," I answered, giving her a hug. "How could you get along without us?"

"I've gotten along fine living on my own for the past two hundred years. Why should now be different?" *Whoa,* I thought. *Something's very weird here.*

"I know what's bothering you," I said cheerfully. "You're worried that we didn't bring you a present. Well, you're wrong." Gogol flashed me a what-are-you-talking-about look. I just smiled back. "Here's a real Alzorian gourmet treat," I said as I reached into my pack. "Roasted bugs. Just shake them on your favorite foods. Gives things a nice crunchy taste."

"Ugh," said Dr. A.

"That was kind of my feeling," I admitted. "But Gogol's mother's crazy about them. Whipped this batch up especially for me. Oops, I mean you."

"That's okay, Arms," said Dr. Autonomou, softening a little. "I have no problem with you keeping them."

"Maybe you could use them when you vacation on Hookem. I hear fish love them." Dr. A's head fell to her chest. "You are going, aren't you?"

"No, I won't be going to Hookem," she said.

"What?" said Gogol. "You love it there."

"I've decided to retire. Leave Roma. Go into exile. Be done with all this. I've caused enough trouble already."

"WHAT?" Gogol and I yelled.

"You can't." Gogol gasped. "I have to get to Earth again!"

"You *have* to?" asked Dr. A suspiciously.

63

"Just kidding," I said, elbowing Gogol in the stomach with both my left arms. "Look, Doctor, you're not thinking clearly. Maybe you don't feel well."

"Just old," she said.

"But to abandon everything you've worked for for two hundred years just when you've begun to be successful," said Gogol.

"Ha!" The doctor sneered.

"Tallulah," I said calmly, sitting down beside her, "something happened while we were gone. Something that scared you. What was it?"

"I—I—I tried to go to Earth," Dr. Autonomou admitted.

"YOU WHAT? But you're tooo—um . . . important. We can't risk you."

"You were about to say 'too old.' Weren't you, Arms?"

"Well, traveling that many parsnits through space is pretty hard on the body," said Gogol, trying to help me. "Not that you couldn't do it."

"But I couldn't. I set the coordinates. Got everything ready. Turned on the OTTO-pilot. Set the time of my return."

"Sounds good," said Gogol. "What happened?"

"OTTO refused to let me leave the room. He and the computer shut me down. Said I was too old! OTTO even told a joke about it. A bad one."

I looked around the lab. "So where is he?" Autonomou pointed to her workbench. The little autopilot droid

64

was in a million pieces. A large crenellated torque wrench lay next to him.

"OTTO's taking a time-out," Dr. A muttered.

"Oh," I said.

"Look, Doctor," said Gogol. "I don't know why all that happened. I only know there is no one else in this universe who can summon up a wormhole to Earth and get life-forms there and back again in one piece. And that has nothing to do with age. That has to do with brains. And courage. And heart."

"And to prove how great you are," I piped up, "why don't you send us both to Earth? It will make you feel so much better." At that Dr. Autonomou seemed to come out of the kind of sad trance she'd been in.

"So that's what this little visit is all about?" she snapped. It felt good to have her back to her old—oops, I mean—usual self! Gogol fell to his knees in front of her.

"Doctor, I've never begged you for anything in my life. But I'm begging now. Please, send me to Earth."

"Why?" As Gogol filled the doctor in on all our adventures on Alzor—the BRAIN, the BRAIN parts, Yada-Yada—I grabbed the basketball off the Earthling artifact shelf and kept myself occupied by running up and down the lab, smacking the orange sphere into the ground.

"Arms! Cut that out!" ordered Autonomou.

"Anything. Anything you want." I smiled. "Just send us to Earth."

"What do you think, OTTO?" Autonomou asked the

65

pile of rubble. Then she shook her head. "Why am I asking you, you traitor? Okay, Gogol, I'll do it. But you better find what you're looking for, because this is the very last time you're going within a hundred thousand parsnits of that planet. Understand?"

"Completely," said Gogol, grinning ear to ear.

"I mean it!" said the doctor. "I'm retiring as soon as you get home!"

"If you really do retire, can I keep the basketball?" I threw the ball across the lab and right through the hoop. "Home run!" I squealed.

11

Gogol

All the preparations for travel went smoothly, and finally the wormhole plunked us out carelessly onto a cold, hard surface. Instinctively, I froze, hugging the ground. Every sense was on full alert as I tried to figure out where we were. I could hear the hum of voices and the whirring of machinery. Slowly I looked around. Arms was lying facedown just a body length away from me. We were behind a low wall and deep in shadow. Carefully, I dragged myself over to her.

"Is it safe to stand up?" she whispered. "I hear voices."

"I think so. Just be careful," I said. "Can you understand them?"

Arms paused a long moment, listening. "No. It all sounds like gibberish. How about you?"

"Not a thing. Try setting your pan-tawky translator to automatic mode," I suggested. I set mine the same way and listened. Slowly, like hearing a sound come into focus from very far away, the random gibberish began to take on meaning.

"Not much longer now, Comrade," one life-form was saying.

"Right," said another. "Then I can finally go home and get some sleep. I've been working three days without rest."

I peeked out from our hiding place. Three men in long white coats were standing together on a platform that was bathed in yellow light.

"Arms!" I rasped. "Here are perfect specimens for B.O."

"Righty-o," Arms said as she crawled to her knees to look. Biological Osmosis—we call it B.O.—is how mission specialists transform themselves into the local life-forms. We uncovered the secret of B.O. in Autonomou's lab. It's actually pretty simple. Your DN-Aydoh, the stuff at the core of every being, flies apart while traveling through a wormhole, then reassembles at the other end. After you're back together, your DN-Aydoh's still soft. So you can change your appearance right down to the clothes you're wearing just by concentrating on the life-form you want to look like. It's all just mind over matter. Looking like an Earthling, I didn't have to B.O. My Alzorian stripe was the only giveaway. But orange-skinned, four-armed Arms didn't have that option. As I watched, she began to transform into a human.

"Don't forget to change something about the face so you won't come out as a twin," I reminded her, though I probably didn't need to. We had already learned that lesson the hard way.

"There!" she exclaimed, turning to face me. "All done! How do I look?"

"Good job. You look great," I said. Arms, who now looked like your basic guy in a white coat, smiled. As we stood, I reached over to a hook behind us and borrowed a white coat just like the one all the specimens had on. Then I flipped the collar up to hide my Alzorian skin. "So, what now?" I asked.

"Shhh!" Arms said. "Listen!"

A voice that sounded like a computer with a serious illness blasted out of a cone-shaped thing mounted high on the wall.

"Attention! Attention! All senior technicians report immediately to the assembly room in the Cosmodome. Attendance is mandatory!"

"That's odd," one of the men said. "What's it all about?"

"I have no idea," replied another, "but we better hurry if we know what's good for us."

"Arms," I whispered, "are you thinking what I'm thinking?"

69

"I don't know. Rubi's the mind reader, not me. But if you're thinking we should go to the meeting, then you are thinking what I'm thinking." We waited a few seconds until the men had turned and started walking across a wide flat area toward a group of buildings made of right angles. Then we followed at a safe distance. Just as we were about to enter one of the buildings, the strangest feeling came over me. I stopped and turned around. What I saw made me gasp so loud Arms grabbed my arm.

"What's wrong, Gogol? What is it?"

"L-l-l-look!" I said, pointing. "It's the rocket from my dreams!"

"Really?" Arms said. "Cool!"

And it was cool. The rocket was no more than a big metal tube with four huge engines attached to it. But it was magnificent. Lit up by banks of floodlights, it stood in brilliant contrast to the dark purple night sky. It was gleaming white with C.C.C.P. painted down the side in red.

"What's C.C.C.P.?" Arms asked.

"I'm not sure," I admitted.

"I know," said Arms. "Crazy Cosmos Cannon Pusher?"

"I guess," I said, staring blankly at the rocket.

"Come on rocket man." Arms laughed, tugging on my sleeve. "Let's go get some answers." We pushed our way into the back of a crowded meeting room and took a seat. Several important looking people stood at the front. At least, I assumed they were important since they were the only ones who weren't wearing white coats. A guy with white hair, bushy eyebrows, and a weary face began to speak.

"Comrades, I'll try to make this brief," he began. Figuring we were in for a long meeting, I settled into my chair. "The launch of the *Mars 3* mission is scheduled for a little over an hour from now. As you know, this mission is so top secret most of you have no idea what the other flight teams have been doing, much less what this whole mission is about. Now I am going to tell you. I do this because it is important that you understand and appreciate how crucial it is for us to achieve total success."

The people in the room began to murmur and whisper to one another. "The Soviet space program has had many firsts. We were the first in space with our satellite Sputnik. We launched the first spacecraft to make contact with the moon. We put the first man in space, the first woman in space, the first three-person crew. We were responsible for the first space walk and the first pictures from the moon."

The crowd nodded and smiled with enthusiasm, and I realized that the people sitting around me must have done all that together. "But all those accomplishments were swept into the trash can of history once the Americans put their astronauts on the moon," the man in front said somberly. That quieted the crowd down. "They say we lost the space race. That we are *unable* to handle the really big missions. But I say, *nyet!* They are missing the big picture. Our *Luna 16* and *17* crafts have

71

brought back all the moon rocks we'll ever need. Who cares about landing on that worthless oversized asteroid? We Russians were made for finer things.''

Everyone's attention was riveted on the speaker. ''The real space race, the really big mission, is to be the first to put humans on Mars!'' Startled gasps erupted from around the room. Another man in front stood up.

''Dim the lights, please, and put up the first slide,'' he said to no one in particular. Suddenly, a square picture of a red planet was projected in front of us. ''This is Mars. Over fifty-six million kilometers from Earth, it requires at least six months to get there.'' Arms looked at me and smiled. I knew what she was thinking. That was *incredibly* slow. ''The surface temperature averages about minus sixty degrees. Which is not too bad. About the same as winter in Antarctica. The atmosphere, however, is carbon dioxide and unbreathable. Our cosmonauts will have to wear specially designed space suits all the time.''

One of the guys in a white coat stood up and asked, ''We know about the planet, sir. I think what we are all wondering is how you can get a crew there. It would take tons of food, water, and other supplies to sustain them for the trip there and back. And though our rockets are the best in the world, they are not powerful enough to get that much material into space.''

''That, comrades, is the pivotal question. To explain the solution, let me introduce to you the head of our cryogenics program, Doctor Ludmila Petrok.'' A woman walked to center stage. As the lights came back up, I could see the confusion in people's eyes.

"That's right," Dr. Petrok said. "Cryogenics. This is the most secret of our many secret programs. But soon the world will know what we have done. We have perfected a way to freeze the human body, yet keep it alive. The *Mars 3* mission will carry a crew of three frozen cosmonauts across the vastness of space. Because they will be in a state of suspended animation, they will not require food or water. Once the craft goes into orbit around Mars, we will thaw out the pilot. He will guide the spacecraft to the surface, landing near the supply ship, *Mars 2,* that was sent up nine days ago. As far as the world knows—and especially the Americans—*Mars 2* and *Mars 3* carry nothing but research satellites. But the truth is," she said, displaying a large picture of a small house, "*Mars 2* delivered the first interplanetary mobile home. A fully furnished, nuclear-powered, dare we say 'American-style' two-bedroom house. Perfect for the first family on Mars."

"Family?" someone called over the sudden commotion. "Are you talking about sending a man, a woman, and . . . a *child*?"

"Yes!" came the answer. "Wonderful, isn't it?"

Dead silence fell over the room. Finally, a white-coated worker stood. He seemed nervous, but after clearing his throat several times he asked, "Why a family?"

The bushy-eyebrow guy stepped forward. He looked perplexed. "Why, for the TV pictures, of course."

"They must be kidding," whispered a white coated woman under her breath.

But, in spite of the buzz of voices now filling the room, the bushy-eyebrow guy continued. "People, people. Just imagine the possibilities. The first live, color television pictures from Mars will show a happy Soviet family, smiling and waving. Then the camera pulls back to reveal their new Martian home. It has windows with red-striped awnings, simulated clapboard siding, a white picket fence, and a red front door with a knocker."

"A knocker?" asked a technician up front.

"Yes," the man said, so proudly that I wondered if it was his idea. "A big, brass knocker."

"Just who who will be knocking, sir?"

"The neighbors, of course," he said. The room erupted in nervous laughter and chatter. "Not right away, but eventually we'll send others to live there with them."

"The crew," Dr. Petrok said, "will be made up of a volunteer family." Now the lights dimmed again and an image of a female Earthling came up on the screen. "Lara Stetsinlovia is the copilot and mother of"—the picture changed again—"this two-year-old little boy, Nikolai. The mission commander is this man"—picture change—"Boris Stetsinlovia."

I stared at the screen with astonishment.

"Gogol!" Arms said, gripping my arm. "Look! He has your eyes, your chin. It's—it's uncanny. He almost could be . . ."

12

Gogol

"He could be my brother," I cried when I saw the picture of Stetsinlovia. "But that's impossible."

"What's possible is, he could be your great-great-great-great-great-great grandfather," gasped Arms.

I had to find out more. After the meeting broke up, I joined a group who were leaving through the same door as Dr. Petrok. I stayed several steps behind her as she walked down a series of square passageways lit with those annoying buzzing light sticks that Earthlings seem to be fond of. She stopped and glanced back at me, so I grabbed the same kind of rectangular board with papers attached to it that I'd seen other life-forms carrying, and I tried to look busy. Out of the corner of my eye, I saw the doctor go through a door marked PREP ROOM. I hurried over and caught it with my foot. Peeking in, I saw her standing with her back to me, talking to someone in another room. Taking a deep breath, I sneaked into the room and ducked behind some equipment.

"Everything satisfactory?" I heard Dr. Petrok asking.

"Oh, yes. Great, great," a man's voice answered. "Very routine. Just like we practiced it."

"Of course," Dr. Petrok said. Her words came in rapid-fire bursts. "I would accept nothing less. Now, I will give you several minutes to finish your meal. As soon as you're done, we'll insert you into the capsule and it will be time to go make history."

"Before you leave," the voice said, sounding a little nervous. "How are Lara and my son?"

"Excellent. The procedure went exactly as planned. I would accept nothing less," the doctor said again. "When they wake up, they'll be on Mars, feeling like they've just had their best sleep ever."

"Amazing."

"And you, Boris, will be an international hero. The first cosmonaut on Mars."

"And what's in it for you?"

There was a pause. Then finally, her voice softer now, Dr. Petrok said, "I hope to get a bigger apartment in Moscow."

"That would be quite an honor," the man said sort of sadly.

"See you in the lab," Dr. Petrok said as she left the room through another door. I tiptoed over and looked into the next room. The cosmonaut was getting into a suit that had tubes and zippers and clasps all over it. He looked up suddenly.

"Aaggghh!" He screamed. "You startled me! I thought I was alone!" He stared at me. And I stared right back. I can't explain the feeling that shot through me at that moment. Physical resemblance aside, I felt an instant psychic connection. Like I knew him completely, and he knew me. From the look on his face, he seemed to feel it, too.

"I—I—I—I'm sorry," I stuttered, looking away. "My name is—"

"I don't care what your name is," the man said, suddenly agitated. "Do you have a security clearance for this area?"

"I have to talk to you," I said, ignoring his question. "It's important."

"More important than this mission? More important than the glory of Mother Russia?"

"Yes," I said softly. "It's about your family."

That got his attention. "Is something wrong with Lara? What's going on? You must tell me."

I stepped inside the small room and closed the door. "As far as I know, your wife and child are fine. This is about me."

"You? Who are you? Where did you come from?"

I smiled. I had decided to tell this fellow space traveler everything. I hoped he could handle it. "My name

77

is Gogol and I come from a place very far away and very strange to you.''

"Siberia?''

"No much farther, and much stranger.''

"Hollywood?''

"No, no, nowhere on Earth. I am from Zrom Dromar, Planet Alzor, a member planet of the Planetary Union. It's in another galaxy, far, far away. I am a mutant, half Alzorian and half Earthling.'' I turned part way around and pulled my collar down. "This Alzorian skin on my neck should convince you I'm telling the truth.''

Boris gasped, then stared at me so intensely, it felt like he was looking right through me. "You talk like a madman with a rash, but for some reason I believe you,'' he said softly. "I feel like I know you somehow.''

"Look,'' I said, standing next to him and pointing into a reflective glass. "See the similarities in our faces?''

Boris studied our reflection. "And you think we're related to each other in some way?''

I looked at him in the mirror. Our eyes locked. We both knew the answer. Tears welled up in my eyes. I couldn't speak. Boris looked away, troubled.

"But how? I don't understand.'' He sighed.

"I don't either,'' I admitted, "but I'm getting closer to an answer. You see, the whole reason I'm here is to try and understand why I have Earthling blood in me. It must have something to do with this mission.''

"NO!'' Boris shouted suddenly. "That could only mean that this mission fails somehow. Something must go wrong!'' He started pacing. I could see him begin to panic. ''We'll never land on Mars! My family is in danger!''

I had to try and calm him down. ''No, there is another explanation. Maybe the mission goes perfectly. You *do* land on Mars and start a colony. Then, one day far in the future, a descendant of yours shows up on Alzor and . . .''

But Boris wasn't listening. He looked pale; beads of sweat appeared on his upper lip. He was trembling. ''Oh, no, what have I done?'' he muttered. ''I've put my wife and child at terrible risk. I can't bear it! I won't go! They'll have to cancel the mission.''

''You can't do that,'' I said, as a dreadful realization flooded over me.

''Why not?''

I sat down and took a deep breath, gathering my thoughts. ''Because somehow, I *am* descended from you. That means that if you don't go face your future, I won't exist.''

''But my wife and child—''

''And if I don't exist,'' I continued, ''then this moment, this conversation between us, will never exist. And in that case, you'll get on the rocket anyway. Don't you see? It's a time paradox that you can't escape.''

''I don't care!'' Boris yelled, stomping around the room. ''I won't go. What if you're wrong? I'll take my chances!''

The man was working himself into such a frenzy that at any moment, I expected to see people rush into the room. Then Boris would insist the mission be canceled. And if that happened, what would happen to me? Would I simply fade away into nothingness? Or explode into a megatrillion bits, the victim of an insurmountable time and space contradiction? Either way, I knew I would cease to exist if Boris didn't get on that rocket.

Yada-Yada had said lives were at stake. But I didn't know he'd meant mine.

13

Arms Akimbo

Rubidoux had a lot of serious complaints about Gogol. Always had. But me, I liked the guy. Which is why I decided to forgive him for suddenly disappearing. Leaving me alone and stranded in the middle of a gigunda space complex in the middle of who-knows-where without a clue where to go or what to do.

I mean, once I found him I intended to do some serious Earthling-type damage to the boy. But right after that, I figured I'd throw all four—oops—I mean two of my Earthling arms around him and give him a very forgiving hug. It's a ritual I've seen work on this planet, and, like Xela, I'm very fond of it.

For now, I just had to figure out what to do with myself until Mr. Russian himself decided to appear. *Act casual, girl,* I told myself. *That way no one will suspect anything.* But I had one teensy-weensy problem. The room was emptying out, leaving only me and some guy without a lab coat who was mumbling loudly to himself. "This is wrong," he was saying under his breath. "And it's all my fault."

"That's handy," I answered.

"What?" the man said, suddenly aware of my presence.

"It's handy that it's *your* fault because my friend Rubidoux is always saying everything is Gogol's fault. But if you're to blame, Gogol's off the hook. Which would be really helpful because he's got enough to worry about."

The man eyed me suspiciously, then asked, "Who are you? Do you have security clearance?"

"I don't think I need it," I said. "I'm pretty secure already. Just ask any of my friends."

He came even closer now and whispered. "Have the Americans sent you?"

"I don't know any Americans. But if this is where they pick to send people on vacation, they should think again." Grabbing my arm, the very strange man led me out to an empty hallway.

"You're one of us," he whispered. "I know you are."

I shrugged. "Possibly."

"Don't deny it. I'm as alien to this system as you are. In fact, I'd wager your story is similar to mine." Suddenly, my knees went weak. My heart began to race. I'd found a Goner! Without even looking! I was a genius! Then I remembered a few small problems I'd had in the past when I thought I'd found a Goner but I hadn't. *Say nothing,* I told myself. *Just play dumb and get more information.*

Acting very cool, I looked him over and then said, "So what exactly is your story?"

The man stood up straight and tall. Proud. "I am Andrei Sakharov," he announced.

I put out my hand in the Earthling-style of greeting. "Nice to meet you, Andrei."

"This name means nothing to you?" he asked.

"Should it?" I squeaked.

"Greatest physicist in the Soviet Union? Father of the Russian nuclear program?"

"Sorry." I shrugged.

"Oh, how sad. I understand, now. They must have been keeping you locked away," he said, shaking his head sadly. "Yet you are here, working on a top secret mission. I should think the electric shock treatments would have wiped out your scientific knowledge along with the rest of your mind."

"Oh, no," I assured Socks-are-off. "I'm a wiz at science. Physics and computers, especially."

"Extraordinary," he said, shaking his head. "I guess I've been very fortunate. When I began to speak out against the tyranny of the Soviet system, the K.G.B.

began to follow me—bug my home, my telephone—and badgered me at home and in public. They even took me off important scientific projects, but they never went so far as to put me in a mental asylum, as they did you," he said, reaching out and patting my arm. "But to emerge with your mind gone, yet with your ability to do science intact is simply a miracle!" He bowed toward me. "I stand in awe, comrade . . . comrade . . . your name is?"

Name, I thought in a panic. *Gogol is the only Russian name I know!* "Gogalina," I blurted out.

"Strange name for a man."

Oops, I thought. *Forgot I'd B.O.'d into a man!* "I know," I said. "Imagine what it was like growing up."

"You *have* had a hard life," said Socks-are-off sympathetically.

"So, Socks," I said, trying to change the subject, "if you are not allowed to do any scientific projects, what are you doing here?"

"I'm here to advise and observe. Same as you, no doubt," he said. "Although I can see they've kept you in the dark about most of this project, only letting you know enough to contribute in your field of specialty. Well, my friend, I will tell you the truth."

"I already know," I said. "This mission is going to Mars."

"Yes."

"And it's taking a frozen family with it," I said proudly.

"Right, but what few know is that for the first time

84

ever in the history of the world, the craft will be nuclear powered. That's why, as much as the authorities hate me, they've brought me here. No one knows more about nuclear science than I do. Its power. And its dangers. If things go wrong, we could have a global nuclear disaster on our hands. It could be the end of the world."

"If it will make you feel any better," I told Socks-are-off reassuringly, "the rest of the universe will hardly miss it."

14

Arms Akimbo

Suddenly, a white-coated guy stuck his head out into the hallway and said, "There you are, Comrade. We have been looking everywhere for you. It is time."

Socks-are-off turned and began to follow the man through the doorway. Having nothing better to do, I went too. "Excuse me," said White Coat, nodding in my direction. *Uh-oh,* I thought.

But Socks said, "He's with me," and that seemed to be enough to make White Coat happy. After walking down another of Earth's endless rectangular hallways, we entered a small room with a huge window. Inside were several official-looking people, who only nodded at Socks-are-off as we entered. I could see why. They had other, more amazing things, to look at.

On the other side of the glass were a woman and a baby. They were dressed in some kind of puffy suits with tubes attached. The tubes were hooked up to a machine with lots of pretty lights. You couldn't really see much of their faces. But what you could see was blue—a little bit lighter than Xela, but nothing like any Earthling I'd ever seen.

I'd B.O.'d once, with blue hair, and you should have seen the way everyone reacted to me. Like I was some kind of alien or something. It was beyond strange to have a room full of Earthlings staring at two blue people and no one saying a word. *Maybe in Russia people come in blue,* I decided.

Finally Socks-are-off said to no one in particular, "I see it's done."

"Only Boris remains," replied the bushy-eyebrow guy from this morning's meeting. "And I believe they are bringing him in now." Just as the man finished his sentence, the door to the room where the baby and woman were held flew open. Boris was coming in all right. But he wasn't happy about it. Two big guys were holding him, but even so, you could see he was struggling like his life depended upon it. When he saw the woman and child he gasped.

"Welcome, Boris. This is a great moment for Mother Russia," said Bushy. Boris's head whipped around at the sound of the voice. From the way his eyes were

87

staring hard through the window without really focusing, I guessed that he couldn't see us from his side.

"Comrade Letinov," rasped Boris, "you must stop these proceedings, now!"

"But, Boris, you volunteered for this honor. There is nothing to be afraid of. Russian scientists are the greatest in the world. Nothing can go wrong."

"I know that. It is the reason I volunteered not only myself but my wife and child. But I have had a terrible premonition," pleaded Boris. "This mission will end in disaster. You must stop it now!" The room around me suddenly exploded with voices.

"I agree with him," said Socks-are-off.

"Traitor," the man standing closest to Socks whispered under his breath.

"It is only last-minute jitters," someone else said.

"Yet he is a volunteer," said Letinov. "We must consider his opinions."

"Might I remind you, Letinov," boomed out a man dressed in a uniform that was completely covered in ribbons, "this is the Soviet Union. Volunteering is just a formality. Besides, he'll get a nice big home where he's going. He'd have to wait years for something that nice in Moscow."

"General Kaminsky," began Letinov. But before he had a chance to get any further, the door to Boris's room flew open and the stern-looking woman, Dr. Petrok, entered.

"Proceed," she commanded. "I will have none of this, Boris. Sit down or we will make you sit."

"But, Comrade Petrok—" started Boris.

"Enough!" she cried. "Be a man. Do it for your country! For a home with a picket fence and two . . . count them . . . two bedrooms. I don't care what your reason. But SIT!" With that, the men holding Boris pushed him down and began to strap him to his seat. At first Boris fought, but when the straps went on, he gave up. He just went limp.

"Begin the freezing process," said Dr. Petrok. As Boris's body slowly began to go from its pale Earthling color to blue, Socks-are-off turned away. As for me, I couldn't take my eyes off of him. *If this is the way they treat volunteers,* I thought, *what will they do if they find Gogol?*

15

Gogol

After Boris was led from the prep room, I crawled out from my hiding place and considered my next move. My eyes roamed around the room, settling on Boris's half-eaten last meal. I smiled. Borscht.

"I thought you would be gone by now, Comrade Boris," a deep voice behind me said. Startled, I spun around and came face-to-face with a serious-looking man in a drab uniform.

"Ibba—da—um—eh," I stammered. The serious face pinched together.

"You are not Boris!" he declared.

"Um . . . you know what, you're right! My name is Gogol, and I guess I stumbled into the wrong room. So if you'll just excuse me." I tried to push past him, but he grabbed me firmly by the shoulders.

"You're not going anywhere," he said as he pulled me out of the room. "Guards!" he yelled, once we hit the hallway. Two other uniformed men instantly appeared. "Bring this intruder to the interrogation room!"

"Yes, Officer Badenoff!" the two guards said as each man grabbed an arm and half pulled, half dragged me down the hall. We followed Badenoff through a door and into a small square room. There were no windows and only a single chair under a single harsh light.

Badenoff pointed at the chair. "Sit!"

"Me?" I said, surprised. "No, I couldn't possibly. One of you should take it."

"SIT!"

"All right. If you insist." I sat down. The spotlight in my eyes made it hard to see the others. "I'm not sure what I've done to deserve this honor, but thanks. So what do we do now?"

Badenoff let out a low, threatening laugh. "This is the part where you decide if you're going to play ball."

That was a relief. "I can't tell you how glad I am to hear you say that. I was starting to get the idea you might be mad. Toss it to me."

"What?"

"The ball! Let's play."

Badenoff smiled. "You have an interesting way about you. All right, let's play. Why are you here?"

91

That was a silly question. "I'm here because you insisted I sit here, remember? A few seconds ago?"

"Don't get funny!"

"Okay, fine. I won't get funny and I'll play ball. Where is it?"

"Where is what?"

"The ball!"

The two guards, standing by the door looked at each other. Badenoff paced back and forth. "Young man, we can do this the easy way or the hard way." He sighed. "Which will it be?"

"It's your ball game. You decide."

"I'll give you one more chance," Badenoff said. He leaned over so that his face was just inches from mine. "Star City is a top secret area and you have broken into it. Why?"

"I broke nothing! I borrowed this coat, that's all!"

"Then how did you get in here?"

"I came through a wormhole in space!" I didn't see the harm in telling the truth. "Arms and I were reassembled here."

Badenoff stood back and glared at me. "You expect me to believe that your arms were assembled here? Do you take me for a fool?"

"No, but I'm starting to think there never was a ball," I admitted. Badenoff began to walk around the chair. "And when I said Arms, I was talking about another life-form."

Badenoff stopped in front of me. There was a look of shock on his face. "There are others here?"

"Are you kidding?" I said. "Remember all those people in the hall?"

The man started on his next lap. "You are very well trained," he said. "An expert in talking in circles."

"That's an interesting comment coming from a man who keeps walking around in them."

"Quiet!" he cried, his voice beginning to rise. "Who are you working for?"

"No one but myself," I said. "I'm here to—" Suddenly, Badenoff gasped. "What is this?" he asked. I felt him tug on my collar. I knew he was inspecting my Alzorian skin.

"I can explain!"

"No need to explain. Everything is clear to me now." Badenoff came back around and stood in front of me.

"It is? So I can go?" I didn't care what he thought he understood. I just wanted to get out of there, find Arms, and head back to Roma.

"You are obviously a victim of radiation poisoning. Perhaps you were one of the protestors at the last nuclear bomb test."

"What?"

"Don't try to deny it!" Badenoff barked. "*You* are an anti-nuclear protestor, and you are here in Star City to try and stop the mission to Mars!"

"No! I *need* that rocket to blast off," I tried to explain.

"Liar! You're a friend of Sakharov, aren't you?"

"Who?"

Badenoff chuckled. "Oh, you're very good at playing dumb."

"I'm not playing dumb, I'm playing ball. At least, I thought I was."

"You know who I'm talking about. Andrei Sakharov was the head of the Soviet nuclear program until he dared to speak out against the state."

"Imagine. Can I go now?"

"Guards!" Badenoff yelled, ignoring my request. "Put this man in cuffs. We will take him to Moscow. Maybe the K.G.B. can make him talk."

"The K.G.B.? What's that?" I asked as the guards guided me out the door.

Badenoff laughed that low, threatening laugh again. "I like to think of them as the Knuckle Gooney Boys."

"Will I be playing ball with them?"

The general's rumbling laugh turned to all-out guffaws. "Absolutely," he said. "And let me give you a word of warning. They enjoy playing rough."

16

Arms Akimbo

EEEE-ERRR! EEEE-ERRR!

A terrible sound filled the air! Mean-looking, weapon-holding uniformed-types came flying into the cryogenics lab.

"Security condition blue! Condition blue! Report to stations!" a voice blared from one of those cone-shaped things attached to the wall. The uniforms stood by General Kaminsky.

"What is the trouble?" the general demanded from one of them. The soldier leaned over and whispered.

"This does not look good," Socks-are-off mumbled.

"Condition blue pretty much describes Boris right now," I said, looking over at the cosmonaut's frozen body. "Is something wrong?"

"Condition blue means there has been a serious breach of security."

Uh-oh, I thought. "You mean like maybe they caught someone somewhere where he shouldn't be?"

"Exactly," Socks said, looking me over kind of sideways. "Do you know something about this?"

"I'm not even sure I know what we're talking about."

"Then I guess the thing to do is ask the one man in the room who does know," he said, crossing the room to the general. "General Kaminsky, what is happening?"

The general squared his shoulders, puffed himself up, and said . . . nothing. He just kind of smirked. Then he looked slowly from Socks to me and back again. "Andrei Sakharov, who is this person?"

I felt a chill run down my spine. I got light-headed. Scared. Something in his tone of voice sounded very dangerous. "This is Comrade Gogalina, a brilliant technician, but what does that have to do with anything?"

Brilliant! I thought. I guess he could tell that just by speaking with me. But the general didn't look impressed. "I told them inviting you to the launch would lead to trouble." The general snickered. "I know what's going on here, Andrei, and don't try to deny it. You have used your top secret clearance to sneak in your antinuclear friends. We captured one a little while ago, and I'll bet this is another."

"Antinuclear?" I squealed. "Me? No way. I love nuclear stuff."

"Thank you, Gogalina," Socks said.

I waved my arms in the air. "The more nuclear the better."

"That'll do," Socks said warily.

"Nuclear, nuclear, nuclear!" I twirled around once.

The general shook his head. "You are all nuts." He sighed. "Tell me, Andrei, how many protestors did you sneak in?"

"None, I swear it!"

"I don't believe you, but I can't argue with you now. I have to go find the other intruders. In the meantime, you will stay right here."

"But the launch!" Socks yelled. Suddenly, two guards grabbed him and began pushing him back, away from the door. I stood watching in horror, not knowing what to do. But my mind was made up for me. I was going to make a run for the door, but before I could move, I was nabbed by two guards!

"What have I done?" I asked.

"I have no idea," General Kaminsky snarled. "But you are guilty of talking with Sakharov. That is reason enough for me to hold you. Lock them in the storage closet and keep a guard at the door."

Nice country you've got here, I thought as we were steered across the room. I caught a glimpse of a group of white coats taking the frozen life-forms out of the lab. Socks-are-off noticed, too. "Launch time is not far

97

away," he said. Just then, the two of us were pushed into a tiny closet and the door was slammed behind us.

"Charming," I said, inspecting our surroundings. The place had floor-to-ceiling shelves that were covered in old, dusty, clunky-looking lab parts and stuff.

Sock-are-off stood close to the door and screamed so loudly at the general, I had to cover my ears. "General, I assume the mission has been canceled." His face was grave and stern.

I thought I heard laughter. "Very amusing," said the general.

"But I am the nuclear adviser for the flight! The Central Committee itself guaranteed that I would be able to witness the blast!"

It was quiet for a moment. We listened hard. Then we heard the general's voice right on the other side of the door. "The committee also assigned us to keep an eye on you."

"But I must go to the control room and confirm the reactor settings. General, I beg you," said Socks-are-off. "We could have a nuclear meltdown. You must let me oversee the blastoff."

"The blastoff is not my job," said the general. "Traitors and spies are my business. Sorry, I can't help you." And with that, we heard him walk away.

"NO!" I screamed, pounding on the door. "LET US OUT!"

"Save your breath," Socks-are-off said. "It's no use."

I looked around at the dirty shelves, the windowless

walls, the dusty floor. Then I did what any brave, courageous mission specialist would do. I began to plead.

"Socks-are-off, I'm not who I appear to be. My name's not Gogalina—it's Arms Akimbo. I'm from Roma. Well, actually, I'm from Armagettem and my friend—the one who I have the sick feeling is causing this I'm-so-blue condition—is from Alzor. He's here to find out why he's a mutant—part Earthling, part reptile, like the other life-forms on his planet. So it's okay to tell me what planet you're from. I already figured out that you are a Goner and we can help you. Or at least we'd like to help you. But it seems they must have arrested Gogol, and, well, you and I aren't in much better shape. So instead of us helping *you,* you are going to have to help us."

I was talking so fast, trying to get everything out, I wasn't sure Socks-are-off understood me. "Oh, you poor dear man," he said. "You're even sicker than I suspected."

"No," I cried. "I'm not a man. I'm a girl. I live on the planet of Armagettem. I go to school at Diplomatic Universal Headquarters. Just like you did, right? I B.O.'d when I came to Earth so I would fit in with the life-forms here. You did it, too. You must remember! I know you've been stranded here on Earth for a very long time, but all your memories of Planetoid Roma can't be gone."

"I'm sorry, I have no idea what you are talking about. I'm one hundred percent Earthling, as you call it," Socks said.

"But how can that be? All your talk of peace. Working against tyranny? I thought Earthlings love war and violence. That's why they can't be part of the Planetary Union."

"Apparently not all Earthlings. In fact, there are many of us who work every day to bring peace to this world."

"Roma-rama!" I shouted. "There's hope for you guys yet!"

"I'm glad to hear it," said Socks-are-off, smiling for the first time. Then his voice dropped to a whisper. "And you must tell me more about this Roma and Armaget— whatever you called it. All my life, I have believed there was intelligent life in the universe. And now, right in front of my eyes, an alien! Perhaps. Or perhaps you are completely crazy."

"Look," I said, "I can prove it to you. All we have to do is find my friend Gogol. He didn't B.O. And if his Alzorian stripe won't convince you, nothing will. So use that oversized Earthling brain of yours, and GET US OUT OF HERE!"

17

Arms Akimbo

Socks began to look around for something—anything—that could help us break out of the storage room. When nothing on the shelves looked like it would work, he turned to me and asked, "Got a hairpin?"

"A what?"

"Okay," he said. "How about a credit card?"

"Never heard of it."

"Actually," he admitted, "as a Russian I've never seen one either, except in the movies. That's how all spies break in. Using credit cards to open the door. Of course, that would never work in the Soviet Union. The state doesn't allow private enterprise, so there's no reason to have a credit—"

"Socks?"

"Yes?"

"Can we skip the economics lesson and move on to opening the door?"

"Afraid not. I've used all my superior brain power, as you would say, and can't come up with a thing."

"Okay," I said, pushing up my sleeves. "Out of my way, big boy." Then I backed up to the far wall, took a standing jump—there wasn't room to run—and flung myself at the door. It burst open! "Ta-da!" I sang out as I looked back at Socks and well, kind of, sort of smirked.

"Hello, Sakharov," boomed General Kaminsky. "Going somewhere?" I looked up to see the general standing in the doorway.

"Did you see that door just fly open? Strange, huh?" I asked innocently. The general's only response was to roll his eyes. I'd learned that Earthling ritual on an earlier trip to RU1:2. But the proper way to do it was to spit as you rolled. *Boy, these Russians really are primitive,* I thought. I was just getting ready to let go with a good one, only to demonstrate proper etiquette, when Sakharov pulled me behind him and said, "You didn't come here just to say hello, General. What is it?"

"It seems you've won this little round." Kaminsky sneered. "Letinov is claiming it is impossible to continue the launch without you."

"Socks-are-off told you so," I chirped up. Socks

looked at me and held a finger up to his lips. I blew a kiss back.

"As for this one—" said the general menacingly.

"I cannot proceed without him," said Socks. "He's my number one technician. Crucial to the success of this blastoff."

"It's obviously impossible to find decent help these days—but come on, the two of you, follow me." Just as we got out of storage, the general turned and glared at Socks. "Don't think I won't get you. You and your friends are enemies of the state and I intend to see you brought down! Forever! Everywhere you go, everything you do, I'll be keeping an eye on you."

"Nice guy!" I whispered to Socks-are-off. He only put his finger to his mouth again, so I blew him another kiss. We followed the general down another of Star City's endless hallways. Finally, we came to a door that led outside to an enormous walled-in seating area that looked out on the rocket named C.C.C.P. Rows of wooden boards were already filled with white coats and lots and lots of guys wearing the same drab uniform as the general. The air seemed to crackle with excitement. And I could see why. Every light in the place was pointed toward the huge, enormous, gigunda rocket. And it was belching smoke.

The general pointed out Letinov. "You will join him till after our little show. But if anything happens, if anything goes wrong because of you and your friends, remember, I'll be waiting for you."

"Thank you so much," answered Socks-are-off. "It's nice to have someone take such an interest in me."

"Very funny." The general smirked. "Now go."

"So, Socks," I said as we made our way to the front of the crowd. "I have just one question. You said this rocket is nuclear powered. Right?"

"Right."

"Well, from what I remember of nuclear science, can't whole worlds blow if you get this wrong?"

"Correct," answered Socks.

"Well," I said, looking around, "guess it's time to find Gogol and get out of here."

"Hopefully, there's no need to worry," answered Socks. "We're using regular rocket fuel to power the rocket into space. Only when it's free of Earth's atmosphere will we power it up with a contained nuclear reaction."

"But what if something goes wrong? What if it blows up before it gets there?"

"I seem to be the only one around here worried about that," said Socks-are-off sadly.

"But Boris. Lara. Baby! They'd be done for. Not to mention little things like you could ruin other planets, too. You know you guys are not the only ones in the universe!"

"Promise?" Socks-are-off smiled.

18

Gogol

"Ouch! That hurts!" I yelled. The guards had ordered me to hold my hands out in front. Then they clamped metal bracelets, joined by a short chain, around both wrists. But they were too tight.

"Quiet, you!" The meanest-looking guard sneered. "You will only speak when spoken to."

"But this jewelry just isn't me," I said. Instead of smiling, the guard looked angry and gave the chain a yank.

"You are our prisoner," Badenoff said. "You may as well get used to the handcuffs. You'll be wearing them until we get you to K.G.B. headquarters."

No doubt about it, I was in trouble. The two guards guided me through the hallways of Star City, a few steps behind Badenoff. People stood aside and gaped as our little parade went by.

"Badenoff has captured an enemy agent!" someone whispered.

"An infiltrator!" said another.

"Saboteur!" snapped a third.

I kept a lookout for Arms. I knew if she saw me, she'd create some kind of distraction so I could get away. The only problem was, I wasn't sure I'd recognize her in her human form. I hate to admit it, but I hadn't paid all that much attention to her new face before I took off. When Arms goes through Biological Osmosis, she usually adds some kind of special touch. Like blue hair or polka dot clothing. But this time her B.O. blended in perfectly with all these other Earthlings. My only hope was that she would see me first.

The farther we went, the more crowded the hallways became. People were scurrying everywhere. There was a lot of excitement. Nervous energy seemed to be bouncing off the walls. Then a crackly electronic voice split the air with an announcement. "Three minutes to launch."

"This is your lucky day," Badenoff said to me over his shoulder.

"Funny, that's not what I was thinking," I said flatly. "Did I mention these bracelets are a little tight?"

If he heard me, he didn't show it. "You will witness the glory of Mother Russia firsthand. We're going to watch the rocket blast off before we take you to prison," Badenoff said as he pushed open an exit door.

The night air was cool, crisp, and barely moving, but it tingled with excitement. There were at least two hundred humans seated on benches or standing around. All of them were looking at one thing and one thing only: the rocket. Tall and imposing, it stood just across the way, smoke curling around the base. The bored robotic voice made another announcement, "Two-and-a-half minutes to launch."

"There's no more room in the reviewing stands, Comrades. We'll have to watch from over here," Badenoff said as he maneuvered us to the front of the crowd.

"It won't be long now!" someone near us said.

I stared at the rocket. "Do you think Boris got on?" I asked.

Badenoff looked at me and snorted. "Boris Stetsin-lovia? The cosmonaut? Of course he is on the rocket. They can't launch without him!"

"Right," I said absently. I stayed cool and calm on the outside, but inside, I was pure emotion. After all, I had done it. I'd found my roots. Boris was the link. And I found it incredible, almost overwhelming, that I was standing there, watching as he was launched into space, setting off a chain of events that would somehow, over the course of hundreds of years, all lead up to . . . to . . . well, I guess you could say, to me.

"Safe journey, Boris Stetsinlovia," I whispered. "Safe journey."

19

Arms Akimbo

"Go-o-o-o-gol!" I squealed, hopping up and down, waving the only two arms I had over my head. "Over here!"

"Two minutes and counting," the invisible voice boomed.

"Look," I said to Socks-are-off. "It's him! It's Gogol! Let's go!" I grabbed Socks' arm and together we weaved our way through the crowd.

"Arms! Thank goodness it's you," Gogol said. He held up his hands, which were locked in heavy metal cuffs. "They're taking me to prison!" Three surly-looking men in uniforms stood around him. The one with the most metal doodads hanging off his jacket turned to face us.

Socks wasted no time. "Badenoff, I insist that you release this young man to me," he said. But Doodad Man didn't flinch.

"You'd better do as he says," I jumped in. "This is the famous Socks-are-off."

For some reason, he chuckled. "Don't worry, I know who he is. In fact, we're old friends. I've been keeping a watch on Andrei for years now. And it's paid off. We captured this co-conspirator of yours."

"My what?" Socks said.

"Don't try to hide it," boomed Badenoff. "The state may have to tolerate you because it needs your scientific genius, but we all know what you and your friends really are. Traitors!"

That made Socks really mad. "That's a lie! I am only trying to get basic rights for our people. You are so blinded by the power of the totalitarian state, so intimidated, so cowed, that you are *afraid* to see what is in your heart. And even more afraid to speak it!"

Badenoff moved so close to Socks that their noses nearly touched. "If you had your way," he yelled, "you would bring down our government!"

"No! I would rebuild it! Make it a government that's truly of the people!"

"Liar!"

"One minute to launch!" the mechanical voice called out.

I maneuvered next to Gogol. "Get us out of here!" he whispered. "I found what I needed to know."

109

"Are you sure?" I asked.

"Yes, hurry!"

"Ten!" the voice began counting down. Everyone's attention was focused on the rocket. I pulled the WAT-Man unit out of my pocket and began punching in the take-us-home-in-a-hurry command. Out of the corner of my eye, I noticed Socks-are-off admiring the WAT-Man. His eyes were really big. "So you *have* been telling the truth!" he said.

I smiled. "Promise!"

"Nine!" the voice blared.

I looked over at Gogol and said, "The Roma express is about to arrive!"

"Eight!"

Gogol twisted away from his guard. Together we jumped over a low fence and ran out into the field that stood between the crowd and the rocket.

"Seven!"

We were in plain view of everyone, but no one moved. Not even the guards. Then suddenly, Socks-are-off ran out onto the field and screamed, "Arms! Come back! You'll be killed!"

"Six!"

"Look!" Gogol said, turning me around to see the rocket's engines begin to roar and shoot flames. At the exact same time, the cold wind of the wormhole began to whip around us.

"Five!"

I turned back to the crowd. The general and his guards were aiming their weapons at us! The wind from the wormhole blew off their hats. "I order you to come back!" the general shouted.

"Four!"

"Arms!" Gogol yelled. "Here we go! I can feel myself starting to tingle!" I smiled and nodded, then looked again at Socks. He was awestruck.

"Never give up, Andrei Socks-are-off!" I shouted to him over the deafening roar of the rocket. "The Planetary Union is counting on you!"

"Three!"

I could see by the confused look on his face, he was having trouble hearing me. "The *P.U.!*" I screamed as loud as I could.

Socks smiled. "P.U., yes," he said. "The rocket exhaust smells terrible."

"Two!"

"What's happening to them?" the general yelled, as we continued to slowly vanish.

"Rocket exhaust!" Socks-are-off repeated.

The general looked a little panicked. "They're caught in the rocket exhaust!" he started to scream to the guards around him. "Stand back!"

"ONE!"

The massive rocket rose in an explosion of smoke and fire. The handcuffs clattered onto the ground as Gogol completely disassembled. Above the roar of the engines, I heard Socks-are-off say, "You have renewed my hope, Arms Akimbo." I shot him a Rubi as I disappeared into thin air.

20

Arms Akimbo

"Gang way!" I shouted as the wormhole dumped me out on the floor of Autonomou's lab and I began my B.O. back to my adorable four-armed self.

"What happened?" said Dr. A, running over to Gogol.

"I found him!" shouted Gogol. "I found my ancestor!"

"It was him, all right," I said. "Same eyes. Same chin. Same bizarro Earthling looks."

"We left just as he was blasting into space—"

"In a nuclear-powered mobile home."

"A what?" asked Autonomou, shaking her head.

"They were going to colonize Mars," answered Gogol. He was so excited he was just about dancing around the lab.

"Mars?" asked Autonomou.

"Fourth planet from their sun," said Gogol. "Named after the god of war."

"Naturally," said Dr. A. "But what does all this have to do with Alzor?" Gogol and I looked at each other. Then I watched as all the happiness and excitement seemed to drain right out of Gogol.

"That's the big question," moaned Gogol, plunking himself down in Autonomou's computer chair. It wheezed. "I've been all the way to Earth."

"And back," I clarified.

"Okay," said Gogol. "I've been all the way to Earth and back, looked my ancestor right in the eye, even talked to the guy. And I don't know much more than before I left. Come on, Arms, we're leaving."

"Leaving?" I said. "We just got here. Don't you want to rest for a bit? Have a nice *decent* meal? No bugs?"

"There's no time," said Gogol. "We've got to get back and find Yada-Yada. Ask him what we do now."

"Roma-rama!" I squealed.

"Really?" said Gogol.

"Oh, yes. I have this very sure inner feeling that Yada-Yada can be found skliing down Mount Opticus. I think we should join him there."

"Good try, Arms, but he said if we needed him he'd be in the Encrusted Caverns." Then, before I could answer, Gogol got up, hugged Autonomou good-bye, and said, "We're ready now."

"For what?" Dr. Autonomou asked.

"To be sent back to Alzor through a wormhole."

"Excuse me, young man, but there's a perfectly good space roamer leaving every ikron on the ikron."

"Please, Doctor Autonomou," Gogol pleaded. "There isn't time. And no one is supposed to know we're here. And—"

"All right. All right," said the doctor. "But only because I care."

"You do?" asked Gogol, going all googly-eyed.

"Don't go snivelly on me now," barked Dr. A. "Just get in the middle of the lab."

"And get ready to rock 'n' Roma!" I squealed.

"Here it comes," shouted Dr. A as a cold blast of wind began to fill the room.

"You know, Gogol," I said as we stepped forward to enter the wormhole, "I have to admit, this BATH runs rings around last year's!"

21

Gogol

In a blink of a blip, or maybe less, we were there, in the Encrusted Caverns, second chamber past the Crystal Pool, e*xactly* where we had last seen Yada-Yada.

"Okay, now I'm really impressed," Arms gushed. "What's your secret? How did you know the coordinates to this exact spot?"

"Just a lucky guess." I smirked. "Okay, not really. It was Yada. He entered them into the data card he gave me, along with the coordinates for Earth."

"What a guy. So where is he?"

"Good question," I agreed, peering into the shadows. "He said if we needed him, he'd find us."

"Searching for someone?" a low, gravelly voice asked. It bounced off the hard, encrusted walls and seemed to come at us from every direction.

"Yada-Yada! Is that you?" Arms called.

The low voice chuckled. "No, nada, nix, not!" The voice sounded sort of familiar, but I couldn't place it. Out of the corner of my eye, I saw something move and wheeled around. A shiny, golden light near the floor got my attention.

"Lewee!" I shouted. "Arms, meet an old friend of mine. It's Lewee, one of the lounging lizards."

Arms dropped to all sixes, coming face-to-face with Lewee. "Pleased to meet you. Nice place you've got here," she said.

"Glad you like it," said Lewee. "It isn't much, but it's home."

"I used to see Lewee almost every day when I was a kid," I said. "I spent a lot of time in these caverns."

"Then you had to go off to that school of yours." Lewee laughed. "What's it called? DUM?"

"DUH, Lewee," I said. "Diplomatic Universal Headquarters. As if you didn't know."

"I just can't seem to keep it straight!" My little lizard friend scampered up onto a ledge. His glittery yellow skin sparkled like the gems on the walls. He stood on his back two feet and got right to the point. "You've come back to see that Yada-yada-yada fella, right? He told me you'd be back."

"You know where he is?" Arms asked.

"Yes, I do," answered the golden lizard. "Stay here, I'll fetch." He ran straight down the wall and into the shadows.

"Great!" said Arms.

"Hope Yada-Yada's in the mood to help us again," I mumbled.

"Of course, he is," said Arms. "Why wouldn't he be?"

"Because he's gone!" we heard Lewee say as he came back into the light.

"What do you mean, Yada-Yada is gone?" I asked, beginning to feel a little sick.

"He told me exactly where he would be and he's not there now."

Arms threw up her hands. "You're supposed to be a brainy type, Lewee. Any suggestions about what to do?"

"We wait a bit," Lewee suggested, making himself comfortable on the ledge again. "Snack?"

"Anything from the garden?" Arms said, sitting on a nearby rock. "I'm starving!"

"Garden, sure. We have dried wheetle beetles, risen rose bugs, and crunchy veggie roll-ups."

"I'm afraid to ask, but what's a roll-up?"

"Big delectable bug, all rolled up. Soft inside, crunchy on the outside."

"PASS!" Arms shouted. "I just remembered I already ate. Once. A long time ago."

117

"Fine," Lewee said. "In that case, tell me about your trip to Earth."

"You know?" I said, amazed.

"Yada-Yada told me," he answered. "Don't worry, I know everything."

"Gogol met his ancient ancestor on his Earthling side," Arms volunteered. "Boris Stetsinlovia."

"So you're done!" Lewee shouted. "Quest over!"

"Not really. I still don't know how this guy Boris got into my gene pool."

Lewee chuckled that low, gravelly chuckle again. "Ah, yes. Not satisfied until you know everything. Like always."

I wasn't sure I wanted to tell Lewee my story, but figured I had nothing to lose. Going over the details while we waited for Yada might be helpful. "All right," I began. "I know that a top secret mission to the planet Mars—that's another planet in Earth's tiny solar system—was launched by the Russians."

"Russians were rushin' to Mars, get it?" Arms said, then went on without waiting to see if Lewee got it or not. "But their technology was totally backward. It was amazing they could even get that rocket into space at all."

Lewee nodded and stroked his chin. "Bold vision. Poor technology. Common enough problem on primitive worlds."

"In this instance," I explained, "the plan was for Boris and his family to begin colonizing Mars in the Earth year 1971."

118

Arms jumped up, all excited, "I just thought of something!"

"What?" we asked, hoping she'd had a brainstorm.

"Move the 'm' in 'Arms' to the front of the word and you get 'Mars'! Maybe they named the planet after me, but all mixed up."

"I'm sure that's what happened," I said dryly.

"I'm confused," Lewee said.

"It's simple, move the 'm' in my—"

"Not about that. About Gogol's situation." Lewee looked at me. "So what if your ancestor went to Mars? That doesn't help explain how you're related to Boris."

"Exactly!" I said. "That's what I have to find out."

"Yuck! What's that stuff?" asked Arms as she walked over to the cave wall behind me.

Lewee jumped up on my shoulder. "What are you talking about?" I asked as we followed.

"This glob of gooey green stuff," she said pointing with three hands. "I was looking at the wall—no offense, Gogol, I was listening, really—and all of a sudden it began to twitch and grow."

"It's a voice print!" Lewee said. "It's sensitive to vibrations in the air. Our conversation must have awakened it."

Arms tilted her head. "A voice print?"

"I've heard of them but never actually seen one," I said, holding my face just inches from the quivering mass. "It's basically a wad of spit that holds sound."

"Gross. What kind of species leaves those?"

"I'm not sure," I said. "Touch it."

"Yeecch!" Arms backed away from the wall. "No way!"

I let out a laugh. "It's okay, that's how you release the voice message that's trapped inside. Here, I'll do it." I reached out slowly, with my finger extended, and gave the blob a little poke.

"Yeecch, yeecch, and double yeecch!" Arms squealed. I smiled at her and took a quick look at my finger. I was a little relieved to see that nothing had stuck to it.

The sound waves started to escape right away. "Greetings, Gogol and Arms Akimbo," a voice said. It was Yada!

"Hi, Yada!" Arms said with a big four-arm wave.

Lewee shook his head and smiled. "He can't hear or see you, Arms. This is a one-way spit wad."

"Oh."

Sound waves continued to spill out of the viscous mass. "Leave in a hurry, have to I did. Explain I cannot, but there is much danger. Others may know you went to Earth. Must be very careful. Much danger, there is."

Arms and I looked at each other. She looked calmer than I felt. There was a huge knot growing in my stomach.

Yada's voice went on. "I know you want answers to the final question. How did the Earthlings and Alzorians end up in the same gene pool? The key is in your assumptions. Examine them. Deconstruct them. Challenge your brain."

Suddenly, the cavern fell quiet. The last of the shrunken spit wad evaporated off the wall. "That's it?"

120

Arms said, flabbergasted. "That's all the help he could manage? What did he mean?"

"I'm not sure, Arms," I said sadly, turning away from the wall. "All I know is I feel terrible."

"Terrible?" echoed Arms. "Why?"

"Look, Yada-Yada obviously had to leave the caverns in a hurry. Maybe someone was chasing him. Maybe whatever this danger is he keeps warning us about has affected him, too." I was so wrought up I couldn't even look Arms in the face. "Maybe it's time to call this whole thing off. Wait for a better time."

"If there is one," mumbled Lewee.

"Hey, big guy," said Arms, wheeling me around. "Now is not the moment to go into your pity-Gogol mode. That's how you were when I met you and, believe me, it's not a pretty sight."

"Yeah, right. You tell him," yelled Lewee, jumping onto her shoulder. "You let that Yada guy take care of himself!"

"Look," said Arms, shaking me hard. "You have no idea what happened to Yada. Maybe he's just fond of spit balls."

"I doubt it. And I could be putting you in danger, Arms."

"Gogol, the only thing you've done that's dangerous to me is forcing me to sit around your house eating fly soup!" Arms looked right in my eyes. "Don't you remember? We're mission-specialists-in-training. The best of the best in the whole Planetary Union. Remem-

121

ber our motto? Space Rangers from a planet of rock! Brave! Strong!''

"And stupid," I muttered.

"That's us!" Arms grinned. "We can't give up now."

"Listen to her," whispered Lewee gently. "I've known you since you were a little boy. There hasn't been a day of your life when you weren't plagued by this question. You're so close now. If you let fear make you back down, you'll never become the man you could be."

"Wow!" said Arms, giving Lewee the high five—or in Arms's case, twenty-four—Rubi had taught her was an Earthling ritual.

"Guess you two are convinced I'd be a fool to back out now."

"We call 'em like we see 'em," said Arms.

"So we'll keep going," I mumbled.

"You mean it?" asked Arms.

"The alternative seems even worse," I confessed.

"Rockin' Roma-rama!" Arms squealed with delight. "Let's get moving!"

I shrugged. "But where? We're at a dead end."

"That's just when things get interesting!" squealed Arms. She reached out and scratched Lewee behind the gills. "I think we should start by challenging the BRAIN."

22

Gogol

"I don't think this is what Yada-Yada meant, Arms!"
I said as we ran up the ramp to the BRAIN Center. "I
think he meant we were supposed to use *our* brains."

"It doesn't matter, Gogol. I have a few things I want
to ask this guy."

"He's not going to agree to see us a second time," I
pointed out. Before Arms could say anything else, we were
standing in front of the same desk lizard we'd seen before.

"Who's there?" he asked, without looking up.

"Arms Akimbo and Gogol, here to see the BRAIN,"
Arms announced.

The desk lizard raised his head and sneered. "He's already seen you."

"Oh, that's right," I said, turning to leave. "Sorry to bother you." Arms grabbed me by the collar, two sleeves, and a belt loop.

"This is important," she said. "We have information the BRAIN will want."

The lizard sniffed loudly and licked his snout. "Impossible! The BRAIN knows everything. That's why he is so powerful and respected. No one can stump the BRAIN."

"If that's true, prove it. Ask him if he knows about Boris Stetsinlovia," Arms challenged the clerk. I didn't think the guy would fall for it. He looked at Arms for several seconds with his eyes stuck open. Arms stared him down.

He blinked. "Wait here," he said, slinking through a door.

"Arms, what are you doing?" I asked.

"Bluffing my way in, Gogol. Play along."

"But, what if—"

"Relax, Gogol. You worry too much," Arms chided.

The desk lizard re-entered the room. "The BRAIN will see you now," he said to my surprise. And his, too, judging by his tone of voice. *All right, Arms,* I thought. The lizard pressed a button on his desk, and the door to the BRAIN's chamber opened silently. Arms and I looked at each other and hurried inside. The frilled lizard with the feathered hat was there in all his splendor. But I also sensed an odd kind of tension in the air.

124

The BRAIN's frill was trembling as he swayed back and forth.

"I am the great and powerful BRAIN," he announced. "Who dares to suggest they know something that I do not?"

"I do, your braininess," Arms said, bowing her head. "I am Arms Akimbo, life-form from planet Armagettem, student at DUH."

"Silence!" the frilled lizard roared. "I am the great and powerful BRAIN. I know all that. I even know what you had for breakfast."

"Not enough," muttered Arms under her breath. Then she looked right at the BRAIN. "Then allow me to get right to the point. What do you know about an Earthling named Boris Stetsinlovia?" Suddenly the hum in the room got louder. The BRAIN closed his eyes, as if deep in thought. The tubes that connected him to the crystal computers throbbed with colored light. Then, just as suddenly, he straightened up and spoke clearly and evenly.

"Search complete. Boris Stetsinlovia. Human life-form from planet Earth. Space explorer. Left Earth at age thirty-two to explore and colonize Mars, the fourth planet from Earth's sun." The BRAIN looked at us both. "See? I told you I would know. Now leave, you're wasting my time."

"Wasting your time?" I said, finding my courage again. "I don't think so. Keep going, BRAIN. Tell us more about Boris."

The frilled lizard seemed to grow larger. "Have you

125

no respect?" he screamed. "I am the great and power-ful—"

"I know, I know. But if you're really that great, you must know what happened when Boris got to Mars," I said, challenging him again. I couldn't believe I was talking to the BRAIN this way. It went against every-thing I had been taught as a child. Then again, if I was ever going to get any answers . . .

I smiled at the BRAIN. "Or maybe you don't know."

"Of course I know! I am the great and powerful . . . oh, never mind. But the information you seek is unim-portant, uninteresting, and unavailable to you."

"You were right, Gogol," Arms said, slapping me on the back with two hands. "He's covering up."

"Sure looks that way."

"Frankly, I'm disappointed," Arms said, taunting him. "The famous BRAIN of Alzor. Can't admit that we know more than he does. Let's go."

"But, Arms, I think he might—"

"Play along," Arms whispered as we turned and headed for the door. I could hear the BRAIN clicking and humming behind us, but he didn't say a word. As we started to walk through the door, I thought our little bluff had failed.

Then, unexpectedly, the BRAIN yelled, "Wait! Come back!" Arms gave me a little smile as we turned around. "Know more than me, indeed. For your information, Earth year 1971 was a time of great disturbances across

126

the surface of Mars. Huge dust storms, the biggest ever, raged for months.''

''But what about Boris?'' I asked.

''The first Russian spacecraft, called *Mars 2* reached Mars,'' the BRAIN said.

''The supply ship!'' Arms said.

''But because of the storms, no radio transmissions were received. A few days later, *Mars 3* with Boris Stetsinlovia and two other family members, also landed on the surface.''

''He made it!'' I shouted.

''That's our boy!'' Arms said.

But the BRAIN wasn't done. ''However, communication with Earth lasted only a few seconds. Then nothing was ever heard from them again. It was assumed all perished in a crash landing.''

''Impossible!'' I blurted out. ''Your information must be wrong! They had to make it!''

''Gogol!'' Arms said, jumping up and down. ''I've got it! I've figured it out!''

I didn't pay any attention to her. Instead, I looked at the BRAIN and shouted, ''I am living proof Boris did not die on Mars!''

Arms pulled me aside. ''Excuse us, brainy. I need a moment with my pal.'' She looked straight at me and in a low voice said, ''Think about it, Gogol. What could cause a dust storm that big on the surface of Mars?''

''Wind. What's your point?''

''My point, mister prickly, in one word is WORM-HOLE! What if the dust storm was caused by a giant wormhole that was stuck open or a flurry of worm-holes?"

"Is that possible?"

"Just put two and twenty-three point six together and it is. I bet Boris and company happened to show up just as a big old wormhole was hop, skip, and jumping around Mars," she said excitedly.

"And if they got scooped up into it, the wormhole could have dropped them off . . ."

"On Alzor!" we shouted together.

"Works for me!" Arms said, turning back to face the BRAIN. "Now, Mister Know-it-all. One more question. Did there happen to be a lot of natural intergalactic wormhole activity around Mars at that time?"

I held my breath as the BRAIN searched for the answer. "Confirmed. A wormhole cluster was actively sweeping the planet."

"That's it!" I exclaimed as Arms and I began to dance around the room. Suddenly, a loud, screeching alarm split the air! The lights in the room began to flash and the BRAIN's voice turned hostile. "You have accessed secret information against all warnings of the BRAIN."

"I think now would be a good time to go, Arms," I said, taking a giant step back. As I did, the walls around the room began to lift like one huge curtain. There behind them, stood an army of big, bulky, spike-skinned, nasty-looking, three-horned lizards.

"What's going on, Gogol?" Arms said nervously. "Who are those guys?"

"Dragoons!" I gasped, scarcely believing my eyes. "I thought they were just something parents made up. Like 'If you don't do that, the dragoons will get you.' Alzor is part of the P.U. It's not allowed to have an army!" I took Arms's lower hand and headed for the door. "We've got to get out of here!"

"Just where do you think you're going?" hissed the desk clerk, blocking the exit. His eyes glowed red, and he had a satisfied smirk on his face.

"Gogol!" Arms screamed. "Look!" The dragoons were slowly moving right for us! It was now or never. I looked back toward the desk lizard—and saw a welcome sight: The chameleon was standing behind him. He gave me a nod and dropped out of sight.

"Now!" I screamed. I ran for the door, pulling Arms behind me. The desk lizard's eyes got wide as he imagined being hailed as a hero for capturing me. But that fantasy didn't last long. I plowed into his chest with my arm and knocked him over the chameleon, who had planted himself right behind the desk guy's lizardy legs.

"All right!" Arms screamed as the desk clerk went flying. She paused long enough to press the button on the desk that shut the door to the chamber. Chameleon rolled out under the door just in time.

"Thanks a million, chameleon!" I shouted.

"No ssssstopping!" he screamed. "Go, go, go!" The door to the BRAIN's chamber started to lift again, and the long fingers of the dragoons reached out into the room. Without looking back, Arms and I tore out of the building at what felt like P-force speed.

23

Arms Akimbo

Gogol and I rushed down the ramp of the BRAIN Center, right into the crowded city streets of downtown Zrom Droma. My heart was pounding. My knees were shaking like a high-strung tremolo. "Well, Gogol, I have to hand it to you," I said, as soon as we slowed down. "This trip is turning out to be *much* more exciting than I thought it would be!"

"This is no joke, Arms," Gogol said. He was looking around nervously. "We're in serious trouble. Those three-horned dragoons don't even officially exist. I hate to think about what might happen if they catch us."

As he spoke, an incredibly, hugely loud alarm began to sound.

BWEEP! BWEEP! BWEEP! it went, over and over. Every life-form on the street stopped to listen. They all looked confused and afraid.

"Security alert! Security alert!" a voice of authority boomed out into the air. "There are criminal life-forms among us. Security forces are conducting a search. Stay calm."

But no one stayed calm. In fact, everyone in the crowd was so *not* calm that they went into that whole frozen-with-fear thing. Heads tilted up, eyes locked wide open, faces twisted in fright. And all standing absolutely still.

"Now what do we do?" I whispered to Gogol. "If we try and escape, we'll be the only ones moving on the whole street. We'll be really easy to spot."

"Drop to all fours," Gogol said. "Sixes, in your case. Follow me. We'll crawl out of here."

I squatted down and grabbed Gogol before he crawled off. "Are you sure this is a good idea? What if one of these creatures gives us up?"

"As long as they're frozen in fear, they won't," Gogol explained. "But we have to hurry. There's no way of telling when they might snap out of it." Then he turned and scampered away. Gogol was pretty good on four feet, but with six, I was faster. Still, I followed him, hoping he knew where we were headed.

"Excuse me! Oops, pardon me! Sorry," I said as I scooted between, through, around, and under the legs

131

and tails of all kinds of reptiles. It was a whole other world down there. A forest of feet and limbs. Long, skinny, pointy ones. Stout, sturdy, strong ones. Feet with three toes. Feet with six. Tails so long that they trailed off in the distance. Others so short and stubby they didn't even hit the ground. "Sorry, sorry!" I said again, accidentally scrunching another toe. Gogol had stopped just ahead of me.

"Listen!" he said. I did, but I didn't like what I heard. The silence of the frozen-in-fear crowd was giving way to a loud rolling scream. Gogol and I both stood up to peek around shoulders to try to see what was going on.

"Whoa!" I said. "It looks like some of your fellow Alzorians are coming out of their frozen-zombie thing and running around in circles, screaming and waving their arms."

"It's the dragoons!" he said. "They've invaded the crowd, looking for us. Just by being there, they are moving everyone up the chain of reactions from simple fright to out-and-out panic!"

"That sounds bad," I said. And it was. The panic was spreading through the mass of lizard people like wildfire. It started at the edge of the crowd and swept back toward us. In no time flat, we were surrounded by wailing, panting, spinning, crazy-with-fear Alzorians. Total chaos. In another time and place I might have loved it. But not now!

"Come on!" Gogol screamed above the noise. "Now's our chance to make a run for it!"

"YADA!" I yelled.

Gogol shook his head. "I don't think we can help him now, Arms."

"No," I said, jumping up and down. "Yada-Yada! I saw him!"

"Where?"

"Over that way," I said, pointing. Then I put my hands on my legs to steady myself. "Climb up on my shoulders, Gogol. See if you can see him!"

"Okay, hold still," he said as he climbed up my back. "No good. I don't see him."

"He was over this way," I said, turning to the right. "See him now?"

"No, maybe you're mistaken." But I knew what I'd seen. Then Gogol yelled, "There he is!" and grabbed a handful of my hair.

"Owww!"

"Come on, Arms, there's no time to waste! We have to follow him! He's headed for the Express Belt!"

"Gogol!" I shouted, wincing from the pain. "I know it sounds crazy, but could I put you down first?"

"Sorry! Sometimes I get carried away!"

"Not by me you don't!"

24

Gogol

Arms and I pushed through the chaotic streets of Zrom Droma, hot on the trail of Yada-Yada. When I first saw him my heart leapt. I was sure he was there to save us. But now it seemed more like he was trying to get away from us. Why? Was it all a setup? Was he working for the dragoons? Up ahead, I caught another glimpse of Yada.

"Why doesn't he stop?" Arms shouted in frustration.

"I don't know, Arms. I'm not so sure we should even be following him. Maybe he's leading us into a trap."

"Or maybe he's trying to get away himself. I say we

keep following. He may be the only hope we have of getting out of this mess." Arms looked at me, hope written all over her face. "Unless you've got a better idea."

"Not one," I said.

"That's comforting," said Arms. "Come on! We better hurry!" We watched as Yada went into the Express Belt station, then followed. The Express Belt was packed with nervous life-forms. They were all talking about the confusion around the BRAIN Center. Cautiously, we maneuvered ourselves closer and closer to Yada.

"Hey," said Arms as we watched Yada stand up. "Isn't this the exit for your house?"

"Yep," I said. "And for the Encrusted Caverns."

"He's getting off. Let's go!" Unlike downtown, the station was nearly deserted. "I'm going to try something," said Arms. "Something brilliant." Without giving me a chance to say a word, Arms started screaming, "Yada-Yada, STOP!! YADA-YADA!"

"That was brilliant, all right," I said. "Look, he's running faster."

"He runs pretty good for such an old life-form," Arms said as we sprinted after him.

"Who said he was old?"

"No one, I guess. Just got that impression from the old, beat-up robe, his strange voice, the way he acts all wise and stuff."

"You don't have to be old to be wise, Arms."

"No, but it helps you seem that way." Then neither

135

of us said a word. We were too busy panting as we charged after Yada, but somehow never caught up. Suddenly, Yada turned. That's when I came to a complete stop.

"Arms! He didn't turn toward the Encrusted Caverns. He's headed for my house!"

"Why?" asked Arms.

"Wish I knew," I said as we began to run again. But it was no use. We'd lost him.

"Aaaahhh!" I groaned, feeling sick to my stomach. "He's going to tell my parents what we've been doing. Come on, Arms," I said, taking her lower left hand in mine. "We have to get there first!" I practically flew down the main road to the farm, jumped over the still-broken fence, and was just rounding the side of the barn when I fell.

"Whoa!" Arms moaned as she tripped over me. "What's the big idea? What are you doing?" I didn't answer. I couldn't. I bent down and picked up the tattered piece of clothing I'd just tripped on.

"Isn't that Yada's robe?" asked Arms.

"I think it is," I said, dumbfounded. "But where's Yada?" I looked all around us. "He totally disappeared."

"Hey! What's that stuck to the sleeve?" Arms asked. I reached out and grabbed it, then stared at the thing for a good long time, but it didn't make any sense to me. "Just a feather," I said, dropping it.

"A feather?" Arms asked, puzzled. She snatched it out of midair. "Why would there be a feather in Yada's robe?"

136

"Oh, thank the Moon of Dunder!" my dad yelled, distracting us. He and my mother came running toward us from the house. "You're safe! We were so worried."

"Something terrible has happened," Mom said breathlessly. "There's some kind of security situation downtown."

My dad nodded. "The com-link says they're looking for two life-forms that stole top secret information."

I put my head down. "It was us, Dad. But we didn't steal anything. The BRAIN gave us information, then sent dragoons after us to get it back."

"Dragoons!" my mother said. "There's no such thing. That's just some silly story we tell our children when they're little so they'll behave. It's harmless."

"Well, these guys weren't," said Arms. "They were real. And mean. And coming after us."

"Look," my dad said, "I'm sure there's some simple explanation for the dragoons you saw."

"Yes," said my mother. "It was a play or something, recalling the days of Alzor before we joined the perfect peace of the P.U."

"You don't believe us?" I cried.

My parents looked at each other in alarm. "We don't know what to believe anymore," said my mother. "Alzor is forbidden to have an army, so how can dragoons exist? But you are our son and we know you'd never tell an untruth."

"Well, nothing big anyway," said Arms.

"Gee, thanks," I said, shooting her a look.

"Whatever's happening," said my dad, "I think we'd

137

better get you two back to Roma until it's all sorted out."

"Sounds good to me!" Arms said cheerfully.

"I'm not going!" I said firmly.

Arms grabbed me. "No time to be a hero, Gogol. Those gooney guys were going door to door. Sooner or later—and I would guess sooner—they're going to make it out to the farm. And guess what? This is where they'll find what they're looking for. You!"

"If these dragoons do exist, and if they were to find you," said my mom, "we wouldn't be able to protect you, dear."

My dad put his lizardlike arms on my shoulders. "I'm begging you, Son. Please go."

"I will, if you tell me what I need to know," I said. "Did an Earthling spacecraft with Boris Stetsinlovia on board crash on Alzor? Is that how I became a mutant?"

"Gogol, not now!" cried my father. "We can talk this all out later, when it's safe."

"Good ol' dad's got a point," Arms agreed.

"Arms! Please, you're supposed to be helping me," I shouted. "I'm sorry, everyone, but I'm not leaving until I get an answer."

"But the dragoons will be here soon!" Dad said again.

"We still have time. They're probably still busy downtown. So why don't you go ahead and tell me." Anger fueled my determination. I could see them weakening. They glanced nervously at each other, then at the ground, then at me.

"TELL ME!" I screamed.

138

25

Gogol

"Come inside," Mom said, as she headed for the barn. She didn't stop to look back over her shoulder.

"Mom! I told you, I'm not going until—"

"Enough! I heard what you said. And if you want to learn about the past you will follow me."

Arms grabbed me by the arm. "Calm down, Gogol. I think you won. Come on." We followed my dad through the door. As the glo-lites in the barns adjusted to our presence, the darkness disappeared. The inside of the barn was crowded with farm equipment, seed, balettles of wheetle, and my dad's workshop area. It was piled high with a lot of junk. Dad always said there was an artist inside him just waiting to come out. He said that one of these days he was going to use that stuff to build sculptures. I think that was just an excuse to collect worthless space junk.

Arms and I watched as my parents moved aside a heavy table and then start to pull up the floor boards. "What are you doing?" I asked.

"Patience, Son," Mom advised. The two of them reached down deep under the floor and worked together to pull up something big and heavy.

"Need help?" Arms offered.

My dad was straining so much he could barely speak. "Aaarrgghh! Nope, we got it." In their arms was a thick, irregularly shaped panel of some kind. It made a loud thud as they set it down on the table. Then, they both took a step back and stood arm in arm, just looking at the thing.

"What is that?" I muttered, almost unintentionally.

Dad sighed. "Come see for yourself." I looked at Arms. She smiled and nodded. Slowly, we approached the table.

"Roma-rama!" Arms shouted.

"Wha—wha—what is this thing?" I stammered. The panel was almost the size of the table and had a distinct curve to it. Wires and scraps of metal hung off the ragged edges. The top of the panel was covered with dirt, but there was clearly a smallish round window in the side. And below it, some kind of marking. I held my breath as I wiped away the dirt. "C.C.C.P.!" I exclaimed. "The letters I saw in my dream!"

"And on the side of the Russian rocket!" Arms added.

The realization of what I was looking at hit me like a ton of twicks. "This is a piece of Boris's spacecraft," I said. My knees felt weak.

"Sit down before you fall down, Gogol," my mom said. "And you, Arms. Since you seem to be his best friend, you have a seat next to him. You've come this far, you may as well hear this, too."

I started to tremble with anticipation. Arms was beaming. "Oh, goody! I love a story," she said. "Does it have a happy ending?"

"I couldn't say," Mom remarked. "The ending has yet to be written."

Arms and I sat side by side on a balettle of wheetles, waiting for the truth. I was breathing heavily. My palms were sweating, which I didn't even know was possible. Seeing how nervous I was, Arms threw two arms over my shoulder.

"It'll be okay, Gogolly," she said, rustling my hair. "You'll see."

I gave her a slight nod and an even slighter smile. My dad took a deep, cleansing breath of air and let it out slowly. His eyes rolled in their sockets. I could see he was trying to relax himself so he wouldn't freeze up in panic halfway through the story.

Finally, he began to speak. "In the Alzorian year of 30,476, many, many generations ago, an alien spaceship

141

appeared out of nowhere and crash landed right on this very farm."

"So they did fall through a wormhole!" Arms said. "I knew it."

"That's right," Dad continued. "No one saw the crash, except for the ancestors of your mother."

"Was Boris okay?" I asked.

"All life-forms aboard survived the landing. The pilot, Boris, was wide awake, but the other two were still frozen."

"So what happened?"

Mom continued the story. "My family reported the crash to the government, of course, like any good Alzorian would. But there were . . . complications."

"Complications? Like what?" I asked, barely breathing.

"Well, you have to understand the time when this happened. Alzor was seeking membership in the Planetary Union. We had to prove to the High Council that we were worthy. That Alzor wouldn't be any threat to the perfect peace of the union."

Dad grunted. "But the crash-landed aliens were from Earth and that presented a problem."

Arms was puzzled. "Why?"

"Because even then, Earth was known to be a violent world. And now that Alzor had Earthlings on it—"

"Our government was afraid they might somehow infect the peace of the union," I said, finishing Dad's sentence.

"And if the High Council found out about the Earth-

142

lings, then Alzor might not be allowed to join the P.U.?'' Arms added.

"Exactly, dear." Mom nodded. "So officially, the crash never happened."

"That's it? That's the big secret everyone has been so worried about us finding out about?" Arms said. "What's the big deal?"

"The big deal, as you call it, is that the Alzorian leaders ordered that the Earthlings be removed from Alzor," said Dad. "So they blasted them through another wormhole. No food. No supplies. No map. No hope."

"What?" I couldn't believe it. "That's like condemning them to die."

"That's against everything in the Code of Values!" Arms said.

Mom looked down. "That's why it's a state secret."

"I can't believe they'd be so cruel," I said. I was stunned.

"That's why this is such a closely held secret," Dad said.

"But wait a minute," Arms said. "That happened long, long ago. The leaders that made those decisions have been dead for years. Why is it *still* such a big deal?"

"It's simple, really," Dad explained. "Every leader since that time has been faced with a choice. Should they do the purely honest thing, admit the mistake, and risk having our world disgraced and banished from the greatest union the universe has ever known? Or should they just keep quiet?''

"And that's why we tried to protect you, Gogol," Mom said. Her eyes were moist. "Now that you know the truth, you have to decide which is more important. The future of the planet? Or revealing the truth?''

My mind was swimming. I couldn't think straight. Something was missing. All of a sudden, there was a lot of noise outside. Dad rushed to the door and peaked out.

"Dragoons!" he called back desperately. "They're here!"

26

Arms Akimbo

"But what about Gogol?" I yelled.

"He has to leave now and so do you!" Gogol's dad said. "Once those dragoons find out no one is in the house, they'll come out here to search."

"No!" I moaned, "I mean, what *about* Gogol? How did he end up looking like a human if your leaders shot all the Earthlings back into space?"

The sound of dragoons pounding through the wheetle fields got louder. "Baby!" Gogol's mother hissed.

"Mom, that's not very nice," Gogol said. "Arms was just trying to help."

"Hush, Gogol. I mean, *Baby*. That is the answer to her question." Then Gogol's mom pulled the two of us closer and whispered, "My distant relatives rescued Baby Stetsinlovia and raised him as their own."

"In the Encrusted Caverns," Dad added. "To keep him away from prying eyes."

Gogol let out a sigh. "No wonder I've always been drawn there."

Gogol's mom continued whispering, but faster and more desperately. "Eventually the child married into our family. Their children married Alzorians, and then their children did the same, and so on and so on. Until, over many generations, all visible traces of earthly origins were eliminated."

"Until me," Gogol said.

"Right, Son," Gogol's dad said kindly. "You're the exception. Completely special. Somehow, all the human genes that managed to survive ended up sticking to your DN-Aydoh."

Boom, boom, boom! Dragoons began pounding on the barn door. "All life-forms, attention!" a rude voice shouted. "You must come out!" *Boom, boom, boom!*

"Guess that's our exit music," I said as calmly as I could.

"That could be hard," Gogol's mom said, wringing her hands. "I'm afraid there is only one door. And we've never had a need for a lock."

Boom, boom, boom!

"Until now." Gogol groaned.

"I just don't see how we're going to get you out of

146

here," Gogol's dad added. It didn't make me feel better that he sounded like he was really scared.

"You won't have to," Gogol said bravely. "I'm going to go out there and turn myself in."

"Hey, hold on!" I said. "Are you sure that's a good idea?"

"No, I'm not, Arms. But I *am* sure that if the dragoons think my parents were trying to hide me, Mom and Dad will be in very big trouble." He turned and faced his mom. "You've protected me long enough. It's time for me to face things on my own. I have to go. It's the only way."

Gogol's mom began to shed huge tears. I wanted to tell him how brave I thought he was, but before I could, a cold, swirling wind began to blow *inside* the barn. "Feel that?" I shouted. I held out my arms and spun around.

"It's a wormhole opening!" Gogol said. He was smiling from ear to ear, and his hair was flapping in the breeze.

"Where is it taking you?" Mom screamed.

Boom! Boom! Boom! The dragoons started to shake the door.

"I'm not sure," Gogol called to her over the noise. "But it's got to be better than here."

"Don't worry, we'll be in touch," I shouted over the sound of the wind.

"That's it!" roared a mean-sounding dragoon. "We're coming in!"

147

Suddenly, Gogol's dad ran up and handed him a package. "Take this with you, Son!"

Gogol looked at it and asked, "What is it?" But it was too late. The wormhole, a quivering doorway to the stars, opened up. I took Gogol's hand in two of mine.

"Thanks, Mom. Thanks, Dad," he said. "For everything."

I smiled and with my two free hands rippled a twelve-fingered wave. "Toodles!" Just then, the door to the barn burst open and a swarm of dragoons ran in. But they were too late. We were already gone.

27

Rubidoux

"Do you have them, Doctor?" I asked Autonomou. The whole lab was vibrating and humming as the computer struggled to keep up. Dr. A's chubby hands flew across the homemade computer panel, bashing buttons, swatting switches. Purple light from the giant screen made her green skin look fluorescent.

"I think so, Rubidoux," she answered calmly, "but I can't be sure."

Xela placed a hand on Autonomou's shoulder. "What's the problem?"

"Simply that the automatic retrieval of life-forms is

complicated. Now if you would all stand back so I can work, this will go much more quickly,'' Autonomou barked. Xela and I backed off. ''Computer! Where do we stand?''

''Energy pathway traced. Life-forms identified. Confirmation of code in progress.''

''That sounds hopeful,'' Dandoo the Grand DOO-DUH said from across the room. He's the one who'd insisted Dr. Autonomou bring Gogol and Arms back from Alzor immediately.

''Hopeful, yes,'' Dr. A agreed. ''But there are still risks.''

''What sort of risks?'' Xela asked softly. I was going to ask the same question, but decided I'd rather not know.

Autonomou let out a low chuckle. ''Where should I begin? There's possible pizmo peril, a huge hampler hazard, and of course, always disco-later danger.''

''But I thought you were going to use the break time to fix the system,'' I said, just a little miffed.

''For your information, Mr. Doux, that's exactly what I did. But I haven't been given time to test the improvements, have I? Besides, wormhole travel always comes down to a galactic gamble.''

''Code confirmed!'' the computer announced abruptly.

''Here goes everything!'' Autonomou shouted. Her finger hung above the purple, flashing ''Retrieve'' button. ''Waiting for alignment of the maxsis crom-dimmer with the rayn forst control sim. Wait, wait . . . NOW!'' she shouted as she slammed her finger down.

150

"Wormhole materializing!" the computer said cheerfully. All four of us swung around to face the center of Autonomou's lab. Invisible energy waves pulsed through the room, distorting vision the same way heat waves do as they rise off the surface of a desert planet. Then, the familiar rush of ice-cold air filled the lab. Autonomou's computer hummed and hammered.

"Drag-nabbity!" she shouted.

"That doesn't sound too good," Xela said, starting to panic.

"It's okay, it's okay," Dr. A said. "Looks like I forgot to tighten some loose lugs. No big deal."

Suddenly, life-forms came tumbling out of the wormhole and started to reassemble in front of us. "Here they come!" I yelled.

"Good!" Autonomou said, burying her eyestalks in her fleshy cheeks. "I just hope they're not in pieces!"

28

Gogol

I felt a rush of excitement as I was reassembled from top to bottom. I wasn't sure where the wormhole was going to deposit us, but I had my suspicions. As my vision returned, I was glad to see I was right.

"Xela! Rubi!" I shouted for joy.

"Grand DOO-DUH! Dr. A!" Arms added, as she passed four-armed, full-press hugs out to everyone. "So the gang's all here!"

"It is, now that you've joined us!" Xela smiled.

"But what made you bring us back?" I asked. "Break-Away-To-Home's not even over yet."

"Actually, Gogol, it is," Rubi said. "Classes start day after tomorrow."

"Wha . . . ?"

Dr. Autonomou smiled. "I thought that might happen," she said. "When you rushed back from Earth and then immediately wormholed to Alzor, you must have caused a time shift without realizing it."

"So our BATH time is over?" wailed Arms. "We were just starting to have fun!"

Rubi shrugged. "Hey, don't blame me. I said we should wait another day to bring you back, but Dandoo insisted we get you immediately."

Dandoo the Grand DOO-DUH ruffled his multi-colored feathers. "I tried to get a message to you, but all communication links with Alzor are out for some reason."

"Meet reason one," Arms said, pointing to me. Then she pointed at herself. "And reason two."

Xela shook her head in disbelief. "You shut down the communication grid for the whole planet? How?"

"Why even ask?" Rubi laughed. "Sounds like a typical day in the life of Gogol and Arms."

"It's kind of a long story," I said, "but let me just say that if you hadn't brought us back when you did, we would have been captured by a squad of dragoons!"

Arms gasped. "Gogol! That reminds me. What's going to happen to your mom and dad?"

"They'll be okay," I assured her. "The dragoons were after us. Once we disappeared, the danger to my parents was over."

Dr. Autonomou placed a heavy hand on my shoulder

153

and sighed. Her eye stalks jutted out just inches from my face. "Gogol," she began, "dragoons don't exist. You must be mistaken."

"What's a dragoon?" Xela asked.

Dandoo answered, "They are an ancient race of reptilian life-forms that ruled Alzor a very long time ago."

"But they are extinct now," Autonomou insisted. "Gone! No more! Kaput!"

"Well, I hate to have to tell you this," I said, looking into the doctor's eyes, "but they're back."

She stared at me for several seconds, then dropped her arm and turned away. "If that is true," she said gravely, "it is very troubling and unwelcome news indeed. Wait until the High Council gets wind of this."

"That's not all they may get wind of," I said. "I found out everything about my past."

Xela beamed. "That's wonderful, Gogol."

"It is, but in doing so, Arms and I uncovered a deep, dark secret about Alzor."

"Oh, yeah? Like what?" Rubi teased. "Everyone already knows the food stinks."

I ignored him. "It's something so big that if I tell the High Council about it, they'll have to kick Alzor out of the P.U."

"What?" Xela exclaimed.

Rubi turned serious. "Wow," was all he could say.

"It's up to you to decide what to do next, Gogol," Dandoo said. His black robe billowed as he sat in Autonomou's chair. His eyes were full of sympathy. "Is revealing an ancient mistake worth having the entire planet and all its life-forms banished from a system as perfect as the Planetary Union?''

"I don't think so, but . . ." I began. Then something hit me. "Wait a minute, I never said anything about an ancient mistake!"

"Lucky guess," Dandoo said quickly.

"I'll say!" Arms said. "By the way, Gogol, what did your dad give you?"

"Oh, geez. I'd completely forgotten about it." I reached into my pocket and pulled out the package Dad had shoved into my hand just before we disappeared. Everyone gathered around. I ripped open the top and pulled out an envelope. "It says, Best Beet Seeds."

"Beets!" Arms laughed. "I guess Boris took them in the spacecraft with him. He probably planned on being the first beet farmer on Mars."

"Instead, my family became the first—and only— beet farmers on Alzor!"

"What's on the paper?" Xela asked. I unfolded it, and broke out laughing.

"A recipe for borscht!"

Autonomou took the two items from me. "Well, these will be excellent additions to the artifact shelf," she said, crossing the lab. She stood in front of her collection of items from Earth and swept several things aside with her hand. "They will occupy a place of honor, Gogol, right here in the middle."

I broke out in a smile. Not just any smile, a huge smile. Like it was the first time I had ever *really* smiled, down deep in my stomach and all the way through my body. Even my brain was tingling with excitement. I looked at Rubi. The antenna on his head were in full squirm mode. "Hey, cut that out!"

"Sorry!" he said. "I was just trying to tap into your thoughts so I could find out what's wrong with you."

"Wrong?" I laughed. "Nothing is wrong. In fact, I've never been this happy before in my life. I finally know who I am. I know my place in the universe. It's an incredible feeling. You can't imagine how good that feels unless you've first lived without it."

A rainbow of light from Xela's look-back eye twinkled on the wall behind her. "That's wonderful, Gogol. We're all really happy for you."

"Thanks," I said. "I have to say, you are the best group of friends a life-form could ever hope for. You've all put up with my sadness, grumpiness, selfishness. But that's all behind me now. From here on, it's a whole new me."

Rubi groaned. "Gee, I was just getting used to the old you." Everyone turned and stared at him. "But I'm sure I can adjust," he quickly added. We all laughed.

"So," Arms said, "while Gogol and I were off destroying civilizations, what did the rest of you do with your BATH time?"

"As little as possible," Rubi answered. "All I did was bop around Douxwhop, visit friends, and totally relax."

"And how was the garden planet of Numi, Xela?" Dandoo asked.

"Very pleasant. I absorbed some knowledge, but basically went from one garden party to another," she said. "And how about you, Dandoo? What does a Grand DOO-DUH do during vacation?"

"Me?" Dandoo seemed caught off guard. "Oh, a little of this, a little of that. Some traveling, you know. I counseled some students, lounged around in my robe, yada-yada." Arms and I looked at each other. Our jaws dropped wide open. Without speaking, she reached into her pocket and pulled out the feather we had found outside the barn on Alzor. She held it out in front of her.

"Missing something?" she said to Dandoo. His orange beak twisted up into a smile, and his eyes sparkled. But he didn't answer the question.

What Are the Real Facts?

Andrei Dmitrievich Sakharov One of the greatest scientists of modern times, Sakharov was less than popular with the authorities of the very rigid Soviet state in which he lived and worked. Known as the father of the Soviet hydrogen bomb, Sakharov was also an outspoken critic of the Soviet government and its repressive ways. The world recognized his courage by awarding him the Nobel Peace Prize. The Nobel Prize commission called him "the conscience of mankind." But the Soviet government saw it another way. They labeled him "a laboratory rat of the West," denied him a visa to visit Sweden to accept his award, and banished him and his wife, Elena Bonner, to a small town where total isolation was enforced. Fortunately, Sakharov lived long enough to see the fall of the Berlin wall and the beginning of the end of Communism in his own country.

Mars 2 **and** *3* Just as we said, when these two vehicles landed on the red planet, all communication was lost due to the largest dust storms ever recorded on Mars by Earth observers.

The space race The Soviets set off the space race in 1957 by being the first to send a satellite into space. They followed this accomplishment by being the first to send a man into space, Yuri Gagarin; the first to send a woman; the first to orbit a three-person team; the first to conduct a space walk; the first to land an unmanned vehicle on the moon and on Mars in 1971. As our story tells, all this was quickly forgotten when the United States put the first man on the moon. Today, many Russian and American scientists are hoping to work together on the most ambitious space program yet—putting people on Mars. Sound familiar?

Star City Yep. That's really the name of the then Soviet, now Russian, city that houses their space program—the equivalent of the U.S. Cape Canaveral.

Are you related to Gogol? Do you have a secret craving for borscht? Here's his family recipe:

Alzorian Borscht

> 10 large beets, peeled and grated
> 2½ quarts water
> 1 onion, finely chopped
> 2½ teaspoons salt
> 2 tablespoons sugar
> ¼ cup lemon juice

Combine the beets, water, onion, and salt in a saucepan. Bring to boil. Cook over low heat for 1 hour. Add sugar and lemon juice. Cook 10 minutes. Chill and serve with sour cream or garnish of crunchy bugs (recipe follows).

Alzorian Bug Garnish

Visit a garden at night. Look for the juiciest, crunchiest bugs (wheetle bugs are especially good). Put them in a jar and let them dry out. Pour over borscht as topping.

Rubidoux

"Morning, Professor Toesis," I said in the delightful sing-songy way I had.

"Is it?" barked the professor without shifting even one of his beady little eyes in my direction. The day had just begun and I was already facing major problem number one. The hulking, four-eyed, sulfur-sucking Professor Hal E. Toesis was stomping down the aisle headed directly for my friend Gogol. Not good. It was our first day back in class since Gogol had totally humiliated Toesis in front of the Four Bored Intellectuals, also known as the F.B.I. Professor Toesis claimed Gogol had been to Earth and brought him up on charges. Traveling to Earth is a definite, big, whopping no-no. Reason enough to have you expelled from DUH and spend the rest of your life working in the Bottom Feeders' food line.

Gogol had outwitted Toesis and won the trial. But the truth was, Gogol actually *had* been to Earth. Lots of times. Along with Arms Akimbo, Xela Zim Bareen, and me, the handsome and delightful Rubidoux of planet Douxwhop. With the help of a slightly wacky scientist named Dr. Tallulah Autonomou, the four of us had been making secret visits there in search of the Goners—one hundred seventy-five mission specialists who'd been sent to Earth to teach peace, then became stranded when the Planetary Union's ruling High Council destroyed the one and only wormhole connection.

But no one could know this. If they found out Dr. Autonomou would be exiled and the four of us . . . well, I didn't even want to think about it. Which brings us to major problem number two. Gogol was cleared of the charges, but it was obvious that Professor Toesis wasn't giving up. Round one had been the trial. Gogol had won. But round two was just beginning.

All of a sudden, the mass of purple tentacle-like antennae on my head went into full squirm mode. That could mean only one thing. A telepathic message was coming in.

Rubi, can't you distract Toesis's attention off of Gogol? It was Xela. I looked over to see her two huge yellow eyes staring at me in a think-of-something way.

Why is it always up to me? I said in my thoughts.

163

You're the brainy one. You think of something. Xela bounced up from her seat. "Professor Toesis! Have you heard about the crisis on Alzor? Ancient warrior lizards, dragoons, are on the loose. Do you think the planet is headed for war?"

"War?" squeaked Krystall, the silicon-based lifeform with see-through skin sitting right next to me. "There's no such thing."

"At least not in the P.U. It's forbidden!" rasped She-Rak, the slug-like Bottom Feeder with half-digested food caked on his skin. "You can hardly have one hundred twenty-seven worlds living in peace if war is allowed." The whole class erupted into all the shouts, murmurs, grunts, and squeals of agreement that thirty life-forms from different planets can make. I smiled at Xela. It was a beautiful diversion. Gogol looked relieved.

Except that Toesis wasn't going for it. "I'm not interested in Alzor," he thundered as he drew closer. "There's only one thing on my mind today, and that's Earth." Then he turned to Xela and burped. A cloud of horrible toxic fumes gathered over his head. Everyone turned away and tried to plug up their smelling glands. "And by the way, Miss Zim Bareen. Exactly how did you know about Alzor? That news is top secret."

Xela cringed. "I . . . I . . . I . . ." she stammered.

"She heard it from me," said Gogol as he stood up from his edu-dock. "I'm sorry, I didn't know the information was restricted. Don't forget, Professor, Alzor is my home. I just returned from there."

164

"You're probably the one who started the war," shouted Toesis.

How did he know? Xela asked me through her thoughts. She was turned away from me, but the eye in the back of her head had a look of concern in it.

Toesis doesn't know what he's talking about, I said, hoping I was right. *He's just taunting Gogol.*

"Look, Professor Toesis, sir," said Gogol gently. "We can't go through an entire semester this way. What do you say to a truce?"

The professor got so close it was a wonder Gogol didn't pass out from the stench. Under the cloud of his stinking breath, I could just make out Toesis muttering, "You humiliate me in front of the F.B.I. and then you ask for forgiveness?"

"Yes," Gogol pleaded.

Toesis turned to the class and said, "Tell me, students, why are we all here?"

"To learn to be diplomats, Professor Toesis," everyone answered by rote.

"And what do diplomats do?"

"Hang out in hostile, war-torn places trying to teach the locals about peace," I shouted.

Toesis sighed, replenishing the cloud of toxic gas. "Rubidoux, you've been here at Diplomatic Universal Headquarters since you were five. You and your classmates are supposed to be the best and the brightest in the whole universe. And you still don't know the difference between a diplomat and a mission specialist? Like I've said many a time, I fear for you, Mr. Doux."

165

"Okay," I said. "Diplomats resolve conflicts, arrange treaties, sign papers, throw parties, and zip back and forth from one peaceful world to another. Boring, but necessary. It's mission specialists who get to do all the fun stuff."

The professor glared at me. "I'm not sure taking the form of another species and risking one's life for the cause of peace can be called 'the fun stuff,' Mr. Doux, but I'm glad to hear you know the difference." I smiled and bobbed my head. Nice to be the teacher's pet once in a while.

"Today, class, you're going to see a lesson in real diplomacy. Please come to the front of the room, Mr. Gogol." Pure dread was written on Gogol's face. But he followed Toesis to the front of the classroom. "Face your fellow students." Gogol turned around, his freakish Earthling-type face turning so pale he looked like a Phantamorian. The professor cleared his many throats. "My dear boy, in spite of the fact that I believe you broke the very sacred Code of Values that rules all behavior within the Planetary Union and here at DUH . . ."

"What did he do?" She-Rak yelled.

"She-Rak," I grumbled as I slapped him. Peacefully. "Be quiet!"

All Toesis said was, "Mr. She-Rak, sit down!"

"I am sitting down," answered She-Rak. It *was* pretty hard to tell.

"Now where was I?" asked the professor.

"You were about to forgive Gogol," offered Xela.

"Oh, yes," said Toesis. "Mr. Gogol, with your permission, I suggest we let bygones be bygones."

"Absolutely," said Gogol with a smile. "Any time.

166

You've got it. Yes, sir. That's great. As you wish. Sounds good to me."

"I've got the idea, Mr. Gogol," interrupted Toesis. "Shall we shake on it?" Gogol held out his right hand. Toesis smiled, reached out and grabbed it, then pumped it up and down.

"This is a proud moment, sir," Gogol said, beaming. "I feel like we've cleared up a lot just now."

"Yes," Toesis said, releasing his hand. "Everything is perfectly clear to me now."

What does he mean by that? Xela asked through her thoughts. I had to admit, something wasn't quite right. I looked at her and shrugged.

"You may return to your seat, Mr. Gogol." As a smiling Gogol made his way back down the aisle, Toesis began, "Now, class, to get back to the subject at hand."

"Alzor?" bubbled Squish. As a life-form from the planet of Oceania, she had to wear a special helmet filled with liquid so she could breathe.

"Certainly you know better than that, Miss Splashily. Top secret means top secret. That information does not leave this room. In fact, I believe none of you heard it at all. Am I right?"

"Yes, Professor Toesis," said everyone together in a he's-making-us-say-this kind of way.

"Excellent. Don't forget, this class is called Dead and Dying Worlds 101. So, let's get back to our lessons about Earth." Then he turned and shot Gogol an evil grin that wiped the smile off of Gogol's face and gave me an instant stomachache. I was right. Round two had just begun.

167

They're super-smart, they're super-cool, and they're *aliens*!
Their job on our planet? To try and resuce the...

RU1:2
79729-1/$3.99 US/$4.99 Can

One day, Xela, Arms Akimbo, Rubidoux, and Gogol discover a wormhole leading to Planet RU1:2 (better known to its inhabitants as "Earth") where long ago, all 175 members of a secret diplomatic mission disappeared. The mission specialists scattered through time all over the planet. They're Goners—and it's up to four galactic travelers to find them.

THE HUNT IS ON
79730-5/$3.99 US/$4.99 Can

The space travelers have located a Goner. He lives in Virginia in 1775 and goes by the name "Thomas Jefferson." Can they convince the revolutionary Goner to return to their home planet with them?

ALL HANDS ON DECK
79732-1/$3.99 US/$4.99 Can

SPITTING IMAGE
79733-X/$3.99 US/$4.99 Can

RABID TRANSIT
79734-8/$3.99 US/$4.99 Can

UNDER LOCH AND KEY
79735-6/$3.99 US/$4.99 Can